"You don't need to wrap me in cotton wool, Drew."

Holly turned to him, her eyes flashing. "I can see the truth for myself. Howard never felt for me what he feels for Rosamund. The whole thing was a stupid idea...I might as well go right back to London."

"You're not still brooding about that kiss, are you?" Drew asked her quietly.

She refused to look at him and said in a muffled voice, "Wouldn't you be? Oh, Drew, what's wrong with me?" she wailed, suddenly unable to control her misery any longer. "What is it that makes me so undesirable?"

His hands were gentle on her shoulders as he turned her to face him. "Oh, Holly, you aren't undesirable. Far from it. Shall I prove it to you?"

PENNY JORDAN was constantly in trouble in school because of her inability to stop daydreaming—especially during French lessons. In her teens she was an avid romance reader, although it didn't occur to her to try writing one herself until she was older. "My first half-dozen attempts ended up ingloriously," she remembers, "but I persevered, and one manuscript was finished." She plucked up the courage to send it to a publisher, convinced her book would be rejected. It wasn't, and the rest is history! Penny is married and lives in Cheshire.

Books by Penny Jordan

HARLEQUIN PRESENTS

HARLEQUIN SIGNATURE EDITION

Don't miss any of our special offers. Write to us at the following address for information on our newest releases.

Harlequin Reader Service
901 Fuhrmann Blvd., P.O. Box 1397, Buffalo, NY 14240
Canadian address: P.O. Box 603,
Fort Erie, Ont. L2A 5X3

PENNY JORDAN

beyond compare

Harlequin Books

TORONTO • NEW YORK • LONDON
AMSTERDAM • PARIS • SYDNEY • HAMBURG
STOCKHOLM • ATHENS • TOKYO • MILAN

Harlequin Presents first edition July 1990
ISBN 0-373-11282-3

Original hardcover edition published in 1989
by Mills & Boon Limited

CHAPTER ONE

'AND he's actually had the gall to invite you to his engagement party?'

'Yes,' Holly agreed glumly, her normally gamine features doleful. 'And I can't get out of it because he already knows I've got the weekend off. When he asked me to keep it free, I thought it was because he was going to propose to me, and all the time... Besides, I *can't* not go. All our old crowd will be there, and if I don't...'

'Yes, I know what you mean,' her employer agreed thoughtfully. 'What you could do with is a new man to show off in front of him.'

'To make him jealous, you mean?' Holly exclaimed, immediately brightening. 'You're right.' And then her face fell again. 'But where on earth would I find one? Eligible, available men aren't exactly beating a path to my flat door at the moment.'

'No... *not* to make him jealous,' Jan Holme said with exasperation. 'He's getting engaged to someone else, Holly. No, what I meant was that if you had someone else to go with you to the engagement party, it would boost your ego and make you feel better.'

'*Nothing* could make me feel better,' Holly announced mournfully, clinging on to her mood of self-pity. 'I love him, Jan.'

Privately, Janet Holme doubted it. And, as she looked down at her youngest and favourite employee, she suspected that, as yet, for all her pretence to sophistication, Holly had hardly any idea what love was.

Certainly she had imagined herself in love with the charming and very shallow young man she was presently mourning, but at twenty-two Holly Witchell was still touchingly naïve in many ways, and what she had been in love with had been the idea of love.

When she had first come to London a year ago she had had a vulnerable quality about her that had made Jan take her firmly under her wing, and she still hadn't quite lost it.

'I take it this engagement party's not being held in London?'

'No...at home,' Holly told her briefly. 'Rosamund, the girl he's getting engaged to, wants to have it at her parents' house.' She made a face. 'They're the richest people in the village and very much aware of it. Pots of money... You know the kind of thing.'

'Indeed I do,' Jan agreed wryly. As a well-known London interior designer, she had a good cross-section of clients, but her least favourite was the type of couple just described by Holly.

'All our old crowd will be there. Rosamund and I were in the same class. I didn't like her then,' she added inconsequentially, and then said woefully, 'What I can't understand is why he didn't say something before. He must have known that I was expecting him to propose to me.'

'Men can be cowards about things like that,' Jan told her gently, repressing a faint sigh. For a very attractive and intelligent young woman, Holly seemed to have a blind spot where the facts concerning the average male of the species was concerned. Jan had already elicited during the twelve months that Holly had worked for her that her newest protégé had very little experience of the male sex.

A sheltered childhood had been the reason: elderly parents, now retired to New Zealand to live with their son and his family. Jan knew that Holly's parents still owned a house in the village where Holly had been brought up. She went home to check on it periodically, and at the moment it was let on lease.

'But he could have *said* something,' she stressed again.

'He *should* have said something,' Jan agreed, 'but I suspect he lacked the courage. How long has he been involved with this Rosamund?'

'He didn't say. It can't have been long. She never comes to London and he . . .' She paused, frowning, remembering how often in recent months he had not been available for their normal dates. 'It must have started when we went home at Christmas. You remember, I told you. We stayed with his parents.' She made a face. 'I've never really got on with his mother. I don't think she thought I was good enough for him. Heaven knows what Drew must be feeling,' she added inconsequentially.

'Drew?' Jan questioned, used to Holly's seemingly illogical thought processes.

'Yes. Drew Hammond. He and Rosamund have dated since they were at school, just like Howard and me. I thought they would have married years ago. He's bound to be devastated. Mind you, I always thought they were an odd couple. Rosamund likes the social scene and plenty of glitz, and of course her parents encourage her. Her mother wants to join the local county set. Drew isn't a bit like that. He's a farmer... Very down to earth.'

'Sounds interesting,' Jan commented. 'I like down-to-earth men.'

'Oh, everyone likes Drew, but he's hardly the stuff to make your pulses race.'

'Well, if you feel you have to put in an appearance and congratulate the happy couple, I suggest you do so dressed for the occasion. Plenty of glitz and to-hell-with-you glamour!' she elucidated when Holly looked questioningly at her.

'I haven't bought a new dress in ages. I was saving up for...'

Her lower lip trembled and Jan said hastily, 'No more tears, love. You're better off without him, honest. I never liked him. Look, we're fairly quiet this week. Why don't we both take half a day off tomorrow and go shopping? I need something new myself. Luke's got an important client to entertain next week, and he wants me to dazzle him with glamour.'

Luke was Jan's husband. A solid, dark-haired man of medium height with a smile that could raise female temperatures at fifty yards. Holly had initially found his very male sexuality slightly intimidating, a fact that hadn't escaped Jan. Her new employee's shyness had come as a pleasant change after a succession of very forward young women who had spent more time flirting with her husband than doing their work. As an accountant, Luke had a major interest in his wife's business, but he also had other clients—important and very wealthy clients, as Holly knew.

Two days later, her new dress carefully packed away in its nest of tissue paper, Holly climbed into her small car for the journey north to Cheshire.

The last time she had made this journey had been with Howard when they went home last Christmas. Now it was October. Next year he would be marrying Rosamund. She wanted a June wedding, he had told Holly, sublimely unaware of her own feelings.

Her small foot depressed the accelerator slightly. Surely he must have known how shocked she would be? They had always been a couple, right from leaving school. She had followed him to university and then later to London, both of them working and thriving on the busy atmosphere of the capital. All right, so maybe he had treated her casually at times—breaking dates, forgetting to phone—but his job as a salesman took him abroad at short notice. Anyway, their relationship was of such long standing and so secure . . . So secure, in fact, that she had lost him to someone else. To that scheming, horrid Rosamund Jensen with her baby-blue eyes and blonde curls.

Holly flipped her own dark bob back off her face with a defiant gesture. She hadn't slept properly since Howard had broken the news to her, and she had lost weight. Still, that was no bad thing. She wasn't plump, precisely, but there was no way she was as ethereally slender as Rosamund. But Howard *couldn't* love her, she reflected stubbornly. He was just dazzled by her . . . dazzled by her parents' wealth as well.

She bit her lip, remembering how shocked she had been to hear him reeling off an impressive list of

Rosamund's parents' possessions. The villa in Spain, the boat, the cars ... Howard, of all people, who had always been so amusingly witty about people like the Jensens.

Well, *she* might not have wealthy parents, *she* might not have blonde hair and blue eyes and stand five foot nine in her bare feet, but in her new dress, the vivid red silk showing off her curves, the skirt just short enough to be cheekily eye-catching, she would at least have the self-confidence to *pretend* that she was. However, as she drove, her full mouth drooped and her hazel eyes grew pensive. What hurt most of all was that Howard had said nothing to warn her. Not one word. No, he had let her continue to believe that he loved her. And that hurt, but, womanlike, she found excuses for him, blaming her own thoughtlessness in not realising that something was wrong, in not giving him the opportunity to be honest with her.

But she hadn't given up yet; she would get him back. He would soon grow tired of Rosamund and her parents, she reflected fiercely. So fiercely, in fact, that a fellow driver, overtaking her, fell back in startled confusion, thinking the frown was for him and rather startled to see it on such a pretty and feminine face.

While she might be naïve where the male sex was concerned, when it came to the practicalities of life, and especially where they involved her career, as Jan had noted with approval, Holly was totally competent.

She had planned her trip home to Cheshire with the same meticulous attention to detail with which she planned her working days.

She had over a month's holiday due to her, having volunteered to work all through the summer when the rest of the small staff wanted time off, partly because Howard had also been too busy to take a holiday, and partly because it was her nature to want to be helpful to others. She had seen how busy Jan was, and since they had now entered a period of pre-Christmas calm Jan had been quite happy to agree to Holly's making a long weekend of the trip.

The small village had no hotel, but the local pub let rooms occasionally, and since Holly was well known to the landlord and his wife they had quite happily agreed to put her up.

She left London after the rush-hour had eased, conscientiously ringing Jan first to check that no rush job had occurred between her leaving the office the previous evening and setting off this morning.

'If I had just two more girls like Holly, running this business would be a doddle,' Jan commented to her husband when she replaced the receiver. 'She's a real treasure, and not just because she's a first-rate artist.'

'Mmm . . . with quite a flair for design as well.'

'You know there must be a good-sized untapped market in the north for our kind of service. I've been thinking . . . wondering if we should perhaps consider opening up somewhere like Chester, and putting Holly in charge.'

'Expanding, you mean? Well, it's certainly worth thinking about. Why don't you talk it over with her when she comes back? It might be a good idea to send her north for a few days so that she can canvass around and find out the best venues.'

'Yes, I think I will. I just hope this weekend isn't going to be too difficult for her. What on earth she sees in that—that idiot, I'll never know. I've told her she's better off without him, but somehow or other she's managed to convince herself that he's the love of her life. Do you know that she's been going out with him, if you can call it that, virtually since leaving school? Apart from the odd casual date at university, he's been her only serious boyfriend. It seems incredible when you think how sexually sophisticated the average teenager is these days.'

'Stop worrying about her. You're like a mother hen with one chick.'

'Yes . . . I suppose you're right.'

Holly would have been touched had she known of her employer's concern. She liked Jan and found it easy to work for her. She was something of a perfectionist, and the other girls often rebelled against her strictness, but Holly, educated at an old-fashioned local school with firm ideas about discipline and authority and fully backed up by local parents, found nothing to cavil at in her employer's attitude.

It was a pity that her own parents were in New Zealand. She could have stayed at home with them, and been cosseted by her mother's spoiling. She hadn't seen them since they had emigrated, and that had been over a year ago. Perhaps she ought to think about saving up and visiting them next year.

The thought brightened her mood a little, her spirits lifting a little further when she found that the motorway was relatively free of heavy traffic.

She made good time, not bothering to stop for lunch until she was off the motorway, stopping her car on a leafy back road which curled its way from Nantwich to Chester, tucking the neat little Escort carefully off the road on a convenient patch of gravel.

The car belonged to the company and was provided for her exclusive use. She kept it immaculate both inside and out, polishing it lovingly each week, and having it regularly serviced, unlike the other girls.

She had visited the garage the previous evening, filling up with petrol and having her tyres checked. One of the garage staff had done that for her, and, surprised by his thoughtfulness, she had given him a tip.

The crusty bread and fresh cheese she had brought with her tasted heavenly eaten in the warmth of the late October sun. Beyond the hedge stretched fields in varying shades of dun gold and soft green until they merged into the violet grey of the Welsh hills.

The fields closest to her, empty of their crops, looked stubbly and bare; as she ate, a rabbit emerged from a small stand of trees and sat up on its hind legs looking round, until the sound of a tractor in the distance made it scuttle for the safety of its burrow.

The air, free of petrol fumes, tasted clear and fresh, and Holly felt the familiar calm that being in her childhood habitat always brought.

She loved London: its vitality, its busyness, its unique blend of ancient and modern, its frantic pace that never seemed to slow down. But she loved this as well: this peacefulness and tranquillity, this sense of time moving at a much more relaxed pace. Close her eyes and it was easy to imagine the dull tramp of Roman legions on their way to Chester.

Reluctantly packing away the remains of her lunch, she got back in the car. Home was less than half an hour away now.

The village had remained surprisingly unchanged, perhaps because it wasn't close enough to any of the industrial centres to attract commuters.

Her own father had made a comfortable living for himself as a solicitor in the nearby town of Nantwich, and, although her parents had never aimed to be in the same wealthy bracket as Rosamund's, her childhood had been a comfortable one with a happy blending of firmness and indulgence that had left her with an appreciation of the merits of being financially independent.

Holly didn't look for wealth from life; to be rich held no appeal for her. What she wanted was marriage to a man she loved and who loved her; a man who would understand and appreciate her need to keep her independence and fulfil herself through her career.

When and if they had a family, that career would take second place, but would never be totally abandoned. A woman these days needed something of her own, and Holly liked the feeling of pride that came with her work.

Of course, when she had visualised this future, she had fully expected that Howard would be that husband.

But Howard was engaged to someone else.

It was a mistake. It had to be. Howard would come to his senses and realise that she was the one for him; and when he did, she would be waiting for him.

She restarted the car and pulled out into the lane. Fifteen minutes later she was approaching the outskirts of the village, the familiar pattern of the countryside of her childhood and teenage years taking shape around her. Those fields to her right belonged to Drew Hammond, Rosamund's ex-boyfriend. How was he feeling right now? Much the same as she was herself, Holly guessed.

Deep in thought, she didn't see the sprinkling of glass in the road until it was too late, grabbing hold of the wheel of her small car as she desperately tried to steer it, despite its punctured tyre.

Her actions were automatic and instinctive, but even so she couldn't help expelling a sigh of relief when her car actually slid to a halt.

Not one, but two tyres were punctured, she discovered. The most sensible thing to do would be to walk to the village and ask the garage to collect her car for her. The safety triangle was in the boot underneath all her luggage, but conscientiously she opened it and rummaged for it.

Totally engrossed in what she was doing, and still suffering slightly from shock, she was deaf to the sound of the approaching vehicle, and didn't even realise she was no longer alone until she heard a calm male voice asking, 'Need any help?'

'Drew!' She looked at him in astonishment.

'Holly!'

Both of them smiled, tentative, wry smiles that acknowledged their mutual surprise and recognition.

'You've come up for the party, of course,' Drew commented matter-of-factly. 'Looks like you've run into a bit of trouble, though.'

'Over it, actually,' Holly told him with a sigh. 'I was miles away and never even saw the glass.'

'Mmm . . . I noticed it earlier. That's why I'm here. I thought I'd drive down and clear it up. Looks as if I'm a bit too late.'

Thoughtful, kind Drew—he hadn't changed at all. Well, not much, Holly amended, looking at him. He was certainly a lot larger than she remembered: taller and broader, although it was difficult to be too sure with the ancient Barbour and baggy cords he was wearing. Typical farmers' gear with which she was quite familiar, but oh, so very different from Howard's immaculate suits and crisply laundered shirts. She heaved a faint sigh. No wonder Rosamund had preferred Howard to Drew.

Drew was all very well in his way. He had a strong male face, well shaped with good bones, and an aquiline nose that could in profile give him an oddly autocratic look. Oddly, because everyone knew that Drew was the least autocratic person there was. As a teenager, he had unworriedly allowed the other boys to put him down, accepting their sometimes jeering comments about his clothes and lifestyle.

Drew's parents had never been well off, and when his father died when Drew himself was barely sixteen, he had been forced to leave school and take over the running of the farm.

There had never been money to spare for the kind of things enjoyed by his peers, and Holly had always felt rather sorry for him, especially when the others teased him.

His dark brown hair looked thick and untidy, ruffled into slightly curling strands by the breeze. She contrasted it mentally with Howard's expensive Knightsbridge haircut and sighed again.

Drew's face and hands were brown; not the brown of a Mediterranean tan, but the ruddy brown of a countryman. Poor Drew! He wouldn't have stood a chance against Howard . . .

What was she thinking? *Rosamund* had been the one to pursue Howard, not the other way round. She must have been, otherwise Howard would never have left her.

'Both offside tyres are punctured, are they?' Drew commented, squatting on his haunches to examine the damage. 'Not much point in changing to the spare, then.'

'No. I was going to walk to the village and ask them to come and pick it up at the garage.'

'No need for that. I'll run you back to the farm. You can call them from there. Get them to bring out another spare and fix it. Is this your only luggage?' he asked, reaching into the boot and removing her case before Holly could make any objection.

Rather stunned, she followed him docilely to his Land Rover.

The Drew she remembered had surely never been as commanding as this; although, come to think about it, he *had* always had an air of calm dependability about him.

Howard was useless in a crisis. He lost his temper and put people's backs up by criticising them. In fact, on more than one occasion he had severely embarrassed Holly with his attitude, something which she had chosen to forget.

In addition to her case there was a carefully wrapped parcel in the car, which she retrieved herself. Drew looked at it with raised eyebrows and a funny glint in his eyes.

'Ah, a present for the happy couple. What is it?' he asked her. 'A time bomb?'

'That's not funny,' Holly told him with dignity, softening a little to add compassionately, 'I know how you must be feeling, Drew. I feel exactly the same way myself. But I'm sure it won't last. The engagement, I mean,' she added hurriedly, conscious of the fact that he was staring at her with a very odd expression. 'I'm sure Rosamund will come back to you. After all, you've been together for so long. Since school, really, just like me and Howard. You mustn't give up hope. I shan't . . .'

When he didn't say anything, she rushed on desperately, 'I don't suppose you like me mentioning it. Men hate talking about their feelings, don't they? But . . . I thought it would help to know that—that I do understand. It can't be easy for you—living here as well.'

Howard had already told her that he intended to give up his job and work for his new father-in-law to be. Rosamund didn't like London, he had told her, and Holly knew why. Rosamund preferred to be a large fish in a very small pond than risk swimming in the much deeper and more anonymous seas of London.

Drew had his back to her. He was putting her case in the Land Rover. His voice muffled, he responded briefly, 'That's thoughtful of you, Holly, to think of me. You must be going through a bad time yourself at the moment . . .'

'Well, yes, I can't pretend it didn't come as a shock,' she admitted frankly. 'Not that I'd tell anyone else that,' she added with firm pride. As far as the rest of their friends were concerned, she was going to give the appearance of quite happily accepting the engagement. After all, she did have her pride. 'But I know it won't last. They're so totally wrong for one another. Rosamund is so hard and grasping, while Howard——' She broke off and flushed in embarrassment, all too conscious of the fact that she had just been less than kind about the woman Drew loved, but apart from lifting one thick and surprisingly well-shaped eyebrow, as though inviting her to continue, Drew made no comment.

'I'm sorry about that,' she mumbled, still embarrassed. 'I shouldn't have said anything.'

'Why not, if that's the way you feel?' Drew responded with commendable tolerance. 'I'll have to lift you into the Land Rover. You'll never make it in that skirt.'

It was true, she wouldn't. The skirt was brand new, and very short and straight, in line with the new autumn fashions. It curved very pleasingly along the feminine lines of Holly's neat little waist and hips, stopping just half-way down to her pretty knees, and the only way she could have climbed into the Land

Rover in it would have been either by ripping the seams or by removing it completely, neither of which she wanted to do.

'I'm afraid I'm rather heavy,' she apologised self-consciously as she walked towards him.

Howard liked slim girls. He had often commented on her own hearty appetite and curving figure, and Holly was all too well aware that she did not have the sylph-like figure of Rosamund.

'You think so?' Drew asked, lifting her effortlessly. 'Believe me, after heaving sheep and bags of feed into this thing, lifting you is nothing.'

Holly wondered doubtfully if he was trying to pay her a compliment. If he was, she was even less surprised at Rosamund's defection.

Even so, there was something comfortingly reassuring about the strength in Drew's arms as he carefully lifted her into the passenger seat. As she bent forward slightly to tuck her head under the top of the door, one dark wing of hair brushed his face.

He tensed instantly and so did Holly, not sure what was wrong, until she realised that holding her had probably brought home to him that he had lost Rosamund, and she looked at him compassionately and said earnestly, 'Oh, Drew, it's awful, isn't it? I miss Howard so much, and you must feel the same way about Rosamund.'

The tears she had fought valiantly to control all week weren't far away, but she couldn't cry all over Drew. It just wasn't fair.

'There's no one else in London then, who might take his place?' he asked casually.

She shook her head, horrified by the suggestion. 'No. No... There never has been. It's always been Howard. Just as it's always been Rosamund for you. I remember how you used to wait for her coming out of school, after you'd left... Do you? You used to be there when we got off the bus.'

'Yes, I did, didn't I?' he agreed blandly, and as he moved his head slightly Holly thought she caught that same odd glint in his eyes again, as though something both amused and infuriated him at the same time.

Once he was sure she was safely in her seat, he went back to the car, found the triangle, put it up and then came back, swinging himself into the driver's seat and slamming the door shut.

'Sorry about the state of this,' he apologised above the noise of the engine, 'but I wasn't expecting to rescue a damsel in distress.'

Holly giggled. Howard would never have said anything like that. He was thoroughly modern in every way, and never even opened the covers of a book unless it was a brilliant exposé on some unfortunate personality and very much in vogue. She doubted if he had ever read a fairy story in his life, and if he had he certainly wouldn't admit to it. It struck her that it was a long time since Howard had made her laugh, much less shared that laughter, but she banished the disloyal thought firmly.

'Here we are,' Drew announced, turning into a cobbled farmyard.

Holly had visited the farm occasionally. To her, it had always been an exciting, fascinating place, but once they had all reached their late teens, Rosamund, Howard and one or two of the others had expressed disdain for such bucolic pursuits, and Holly had loyally said nothing rather than criticise Howard's views.

Now, though, she felt the familiar frisson of pleasure she had felt as a girl as the Land Rover stopped and the yard was busy with a flurry of dogs, hens and geese, all of them making a considerable amount of noise.

A terrifyingly loud bellow far too near at hand made her jump, and Drew chuckled. 'It's all right, that's just Ben.'

'Ben?'

'Benjamin Leonard Brahmin the Tenth. My prize bull,' he informed her with a grin. 'He's tied up in one of the cattle sheds, and very resentful about it, too.'

'Tied up? Oh, Drew, you haven't gone in for all that intensive farming, have you?'

Her disappointment showed in her face. Drew's father had grown mainly crops and kept a small dairy herd, and Holly had fond memories of the chickens who had scratched round the yard, and the goats kept by Drew's mother. She hated the thought of the farm being converted into high-intensity units, with battery hens and tethered goats.

'No, but Ben has fulfilled his duties for the summer, so I've brought him in to give him and the cows a rest.'

He saw the realisation dawn in her eyes and watched as her face flushed a warm pink.

'So you can still do that,' he said softly, making her blush even harder. Howard was always criticising her for being so easily embarrassed, but she couldn't help it.

Avoiding Drew's eyes, she tried to get out of the Land Rover.

'Hang on,' he told her, 'I'll lift you down.'

He did, and then, to her surprise, he didn't put her down, but strode across the yard with her in his arms.

'Drew!' she protested.

'You can't walk on these cobbles in those heels,' he pointed out calmly. 'You'll either break them or break your ankle. Put your arms round my neck, would you, Holly?' he commanded casually.

She obeyed him automatically, wondering absently why it was that she always felt so at home with Drew, so comfortable. When Howard put his arms round her her heart started thumping, and her pulses raced.

But when he kissed her all that excitement disappeared somehow.

She frowned unhappily, not wanting to dwell on such unpalatable truths. She and Howard had never been lovers, not because she hadn't wanted him to make love to her, but because, for some reason or another, they never seemed to find the time or the place. Their dates were always short, snatched affairs sandwiched into their mutually busy lives; and on those rare occasions when they had had both the time and the opportunity to make love, Howard had always made some excuse to leave.

Of course, when she had lived at home it had been impossible for them to be lovers, her parents had very old-fashioned ideas; but she had fully expected that this would change once she was living in London.

Sadly, she leaned her head into the comforting warmth of Drew's chest. Was that another advantage that Rosamund had over her? Did *she* have the power to excite and arouse Howard's desire?

Whenever she had plucked up the courage to ask him about it, he had grown angry with her, and pointed out that they had known one another a long time, that she ought to be pleased that he respected and cared for her too much to see her merely as a partner for sex. Making love was something that would happen in its own good time, he added, and because she loved him she had accepted what he had said, although she had to acknowledge with painful honesty that five years was a long time to wait for a man to desire you.

'Something wrong?'

They had reached the back door, and Drew shifted her weight slightly, nestling her against his chest as he opened it.

'I was just thinking about Howard and Rosamund. Drew, can I ask you something?'

They were in the kitchen now, and Holly was amazed to see how much it had changed. Gone were the shabby cupboards and ancient gas stove she remembered Drew's mother using, and in their place were new units in plain unstained or varnished wood, and a modern Aga in golden sunny yellow.

'This is nice,' she approved, giving the units a professional inspection. 'Who made them for you?'

'I did,' Drew told her, surprising her, adding in a dry voice, 'It's something to do in the winter.'

'You made these? But, Drew, they're marvellous! Dragged and then varnished, and perhaps even stencilled—well, you wouldn't get much change out of twenty thousand pounds for that kind of kitchen.'

'Yes ... I thought of getting someone to do something like that,' Drew told her, surprising her even further, 'but I just haven't got round to it.'

Decorative paint finishes were one of Holly's specialities, and she itched to get to work on the clean, untouched wood, but she remembered that she had wanted to ask him something.

He was still carrying her, even though they were now safely inside the kitchen, and she was glad because their intimacy gave her the courage to ask the question which had been burning an acid brand on her heart ever since Howard had told her he was engaged to Rosamund.

Turning her head even further into his chest, she asked in a muted voice, 'When you and Rosamund made love, was it ... was it like it is in the books? You know...'

Drew had gone very still. She shouldn't have asked him, Holly acknowledged, cursing her rashness. She gave a little shiver of tension and lifted her head to apologise.

Close to, the bones of his face looked hard and masculine, the brown skin drawn firmly over them. His eyes behind the obscuring frame of his glasses were golden brown ... like sherry, she realised with an odd start, puzzled that she had never noticed their distinctive colour before. But then, come to think of it, she had never been this close to him before. He was still holding her, and not even breathing heavily, as though her weight were the mere nothing he had claimed.

'Why do you ask?' he said quietly. 'You've never struck me as the kind of girl who wants to pry into people's personal lives, so it must be because you fear that Howard will make an unfavourable comparison between you and Rosamund. Is that it, Holly? *Are* you worried that Howard will compare your love-making to Rosamund's, to your disadvantage?'

She hung her head. She had not expected his comprehension to be so acute.

'Yes,' she acknowledged in a small voice.

She felt his chest lift as he drew in a deep breath, and then expelled it in a faint sigh.

'I wonder—am I to infer from that, that when you and Howard made love it was not "like it is in books"?' he asked drily.

'Well, not exactly.' She ducked her head, not wanting him to look directly at her. 'I shouldn't have asked. It was . . . it was silly of me.'

'But understandable,' Drew commented, further astonishing her when he added obliquely, 'To the best of my knowledge, the only books Neston has ever opened were text books! We men are at a disadvantage when it comes to pleasing women sexually,' he told her calmly. 'We can't always be sure what *does* please you unless you tell us, and you can be remarkably reticent about doing just that.'

'Oh, Drew, I keep forgetting that this is just as bad for you as it is for me. It must be awful for you, wondering if Rosamund . . .'

She broke off, confused and cross with herself for her thoughtlessness, but Drew didn't seem to mind. Quite calmly he finished for her, 'If Rosamund is comparing my lovemaking to Neston's, do you mean?'

'Well, I don't suppose you'll have had as much experience as Howard,' she comforted. 'I mean, living here . . . and always only going out with Rosamund.'

'Neston has only ever gone out with you,' he pointed out mildly. 'So there shouldn't *be* much difference.'

'Well, no. But Howard has dated other girls. Oh, he's always told me about them,' she hastened to add. 'And of course, when he was at university and I was still at school it was only natural that he should be tempted, and then when he was working abroad for a year . . . Besides, men do like to . . .'

'Experiment,' Drew suggested.

'Er—yes.'

'And yet it seems that you never enjoyed the benefit of these experiments, or have I misunderstood?' he questioned with deceptive mildness.

He hadn't, and she could only flush defensively and miserably, and say huskily, 'Could you put me down, please? I must ring the garage.'

'I'll do that for you,' he told her easily, carefully putting her on a convenient stool. 'You just sit there.'

The telephone was obviously not in the kitchen. He came back within a few minutes, his face grave.

'No luck, I'm afraid. The garage doesn't have a spare, and they say that they doubt they will be able to get one before Monday at the earliest, and maybe not even then.'

'Oh, no! Well I'll just have to try somewhere else.'

'At this time on a Friday? By the time they get out here it will be gone five.'

'Well, I'll have to find a twenty-four-hour service garage.'

'Well, yes...but they mainly operate on motorways. Aren't you in the AA or something?'

'No,' she told him miserably. It was something she had been meaning to do, but just not got round to. 'Oh, what on earth am I going to do? I can manage to walk to the village from here, but to get to the party tomorrow night and then back to London on Monday...'

'I've got a suggestion,' Drew told her easily. 'I can probably tow the car back here with the Land Rover. You could spend the weekend here, and I could give you a lift to and from the party tomorrow. Then on Monday morning I could drive you into Chester to get the train. When your car is fixed, I'll give you a ring and you can come up and collect it.'

'Oh, Drew! I couldn't put you to so much trouble. Besides, I'm booked in at the Dog and Duck.'

'Mrs Matthews won't mind.'

It occurred to Holly that Drew could just as easily have suggested driving her into the village and then collecting her en route for the party tomorrow, but she suspected that he had very little free time, and she was reluctant to suggest it.

'Well, if you're sure I won't be any trouble...'

'Quite sure,' he told her briefly. 'Wait here, I'll go outside and bring your stuff in, and then I'll go and get your car. Oh, I'd better show you where you can sleep first. It's this way.'

He walked across the room and opened a door, pausing when Holly hesitated.

'Shouldn't we...that is, will your mother mind?'

'My mother?' he frowned and then his frown cleared. 'Oh, I see... My mother doesn't live here any more, Holly. She remarried two years ago and she's living in Chester now. But even if she wasn't, I'm sure she wouldn't mind.'

'I see. And... and your brothers and sister?'

'All away as well,' Drew told her cheerfully. 'Ah...I see what it is. You're worried about being here alone with me.'

He sounded almost approving, but even so Holly hastily corrected him. 'Heavens, no! Nothing like that. Men and women live together all the time in London now without... without being sexually involved.'

Even to her own ears her voice sounded overbright, although what she had said was perfectly true. True it might be, but that didn't alter her own inner conviction that her own parents would most definitely not approve of what she was doing.

This was the nineteen eighties, she told herself firmly, and besides, she and Drew were doing nothing wrong. They were not lovers, nor ever likely to be.

'Holly, if you'd rather not stay...'

'Oh, no,' she told him quickly. 'If people choose to leap to the wrong conclusion, that's their affair, isn't it? I mean, you and I know that... well...'

'That we're not lovers,' Drew supplied for her.

His head was turned toward her but, because of the sun streaming in through the window and blinding her, she was unable to see his face. Still, something about the soft way in which he said the words made her muscles tense slightly, as though they were preparing to ward off danger.

Seconds later she, Holly, was telling herself that she must learn to relax. What possible danger could she be in from Drew, of all people? Why, only less than half an hour ago she had been thinking how very safe and comfortable she felt with him. Just because she was going to spend a couple of nights alone with him, there was no reason for her to get all nervous and het up.

'Have you made any other alterations?' she asked him as he opened the door and she followed him into an inner hall.

An ancient oak staircase led upstairs, the wood worn by countless generations of hands and feet. It felt warm to her touch, and pleasantly smooth.

'Some. I've installed two new bathrooms, and built some wardrobes in my own and the guest bedrooms. What I need now is a decorator, but somehow or other...'

Somehow or other he had lost heart, she thought sympathetically, and no wonder. He would have been modernising the house for Rosamund, and she felt a fierce thrill of resentment against the other woman for hurting him as she must have done. Drew was far too nice for a woman like Rosamund. She wanted to tell him as much, but she stopped herself just in time. He couldn't help loving Rosamund any more than she could help loving Howard.

'You know, I'm surprised he had the gall to invite you to this do,' he commented, as he led the way down a long corridor linking the bedrooms together. On one side of it were a series of closed doors, and on the other windows which overlooked the fields. Holly paused and studied the landscape.

'Oh, you've kept the water meadow!' she exclaimed with pleasure.

The field in question was steep and marshy, with a small river running through it. Holly remembered that at one time Drew had seriously considered having it drained. She had pleaded with him not to, loving the wild flowers that grew among the rushes in springtime.

'It would have been prohibitively expensive, and besides, I can sell the rushes now. Someone's set up in business in the village, making traditional baskets, and chair seats, that kind of thing, and he comes and cuts the rushes when they're ready. Why did you come, Holly?' he pressed, returning to his earlier comment.

'I had to.' She turned to look at him, her eyes bright and defiant. 'He'll come back to me, Drew. I know he will. If I could just make him see how wrong Rosamund is for him. Jan—my boss—suggested I should find a man to bring with me. You know, to make Howard jealous.'

'But you decided not to?' he questioned, giving her a sharp look.

'Well, I didn't have much option. I don't *know* any men, really, other than Howard,' she admitted honestly.

'Mmm.' He turned away from her and opened a door.

Sunlight flooded the pretty room through the dormer window set into the sloping roof.

'Oh, Drew, it's lovely!'

'Bathroom's next door,' he told her laconically. 'It isn't exactly en suite, but you'll have it to yourself, since I use the one off my own room which is at the other end of the house.'

How tactful and considerate he was. Impulsively, she reached up and kissed him on the cheek. He went as still as a statue, and dark red colour flooded her face as she realised what she had done.

'I'm sorry, Drew,' she apologised falteringly. 'I never thought . . .'

Of course, being kissed by any woman was bound to remind him of Rosamund. She felt exactly the same way and she ought to have realised.

'I'd better go and get your car before it starts to go dark.'

CHAPTER TWO

'DREW, I'm so nervous. I don't think I want to go.'

Holly was standing in the kitchen, wearing her new dress, her hair freshly washed, her face made-up, but all her courage had deserted her, and she didn't think she was going to be able to face Howard and Rosamund.

'You've got to,' Drew told her bluntly. 'Too many people know you're here.'

It was true. Only this morning the postman had given her a cheery welcome, saying that he had heard from Mrs Matthews about her car and that she was staying at the farm. Knowing him, by now all her old friends would have heard she was home.

The party was going to be very formal, and initially she had been rather stunned by the sight of Drew in his dinner-suit. For one thing she hadn't expected him to own a dinner-suit, but, when she had naïvely said as much, he had gravely informed her that he had had to buy one in order to attend the local Young Farmers' 'dos'.

He was even wearing a fashionable wing-collared shirt, so crisply laundered that it could have rivalled one of Howard's. However, as she glanced downwards Holly forgot her doubts about attending the party and exclaimed, 'Drew, you're wearing green socks.'

'Am I?' He looked completely unperturbed. 'I'd better go up and change them. It would help if you came with me and supervised.' He saw her face and said quietly, 'I'm colour-blind, Holly. Don't you remember? Or at least, partially colour-blind. I could spend the rest of the evening up there trying to find the right pair.'

Of course, now that he mentioned it, she did remember him once saying to her about his inability to differentiate between certain colours.

'To tell the truth,' he confided as they went upstairs, 'that's one of the reasons I've hesitated about redecorating. I'm terrified of choosing the wrong colours.'

'Oh, but surely Rosamund would have chosen those?'

At her side Drew heaved a sigh that lifted his chest and made her wonder absently how wide it was... certainly much wider than Howard's. Howard's chest was inclined to be uncomfortably bony, but then Howard didn't have the benefit of working outside, she told herself loyally.

'Perhaps once,' Drew agreed mournfully. 'Although she never really liked this house.'

'I suppose she thought it wasn't good enough for her,' Holly said wrathfully, remember Rosamund's snobbery.

At her side, Drew gave her a considering look which she didn't see. 'No, I suppose not.'

'She must be blind,' Holly told him roundly. 'I think it's lovely, but I suppose Rosamund would prefer one of those horrid little boxy things her father used to build.'

Ignoring her reference to the way in which Rosamund's father had made his money, Drew agreed.

'Yes, I think she would. She says old houses are dirty.'

Yes, Holly could just imagine her saying it, too.

'That's all she knows. Why, with a little bit of thought and care this house could be far more attractive than that awful place her father built.'

'Do you think so?' Drew commented doubtfully.

Resenting this aspersion on her knowledge and ability, Holly said firmly, 'Yes. Yes, I do. In fact, I could prove it to you, Drew. You know I work for an interior designer now. Decorative paint finishes are my specialty. You know, dragging, sponging, marbling...that kind of thing. Perhaps you haven't heard of them,' she added kindly, 'but they're very much in demand.'

For some reason Drew looked as though he was having a problem controlling his facial muscles, probably because talking about the house and Rosamund brought home to him the reality of what had happened, Holly reflected compassionately.

'Well, anyway, they *are* very much in demand.' Modestly, she didn't add that she herself was also very much in demand, as much for her inventive and imaginative *trompe-l'oeil* scenery as for her stencilling and dragging. 'I'd love to have the opportunity to paint your kitchen,' she added wistfully.

She could see it now, the cupboards dragged in sunny yellow, with perhaps a circlet of ivy and white dog-roses painted on the fronts. She could sponge the walls to match and make roller blinds that faithfully copied the landscape outside the windows.

Upstairs, this long corridor just cried out for something jolly and period ... a scene from an alehouse, perhaps. There must be something she could use as a base in Chester library's local history section. Carried away with enthusiasm, she forgot her nervousness.

'It's a pity you can't stay up here longer and get this place sorted out for me,' Drew commented, watching her.

'I'd love to,' she admitted, her eyes sparkling at the thought.

'My bedroom's here,' he told her, pushing open a door.

It was a large room on the same side of the house as her own, but with more windows. It had a huge bed set in a carved cherrywood frame.

'Oh, Drew, I love this!' she told him reverently, forgetting his socks and touching the carving with gentle fingers.

'Do you? I'm glad ... I did it myself.' He saw her astonishment and smiled. 'Woodwork has always been a hobby of mine.'

Holly looked round the bedroom with new eyes, noting the wardrobe and dresser. 'Did you make those as well?' she asked him. He nodded.

But, beautiful though the furniture was, it needed the right setting to show it off properly. The bedroom's walls and ceiling were painted magnolia, and looked dull, like the plain brown carpet and the beige curtains.

As though he read her mind, Drew said apologetically, 'Knowing my problem with colours, I played it safe and chose ones I knew I could recognise.'

He was unexpectedly tidy for a man, far tidier than she was herself, she acknowledged guiltily, and far more domesticated. The meal he had prepared for them last night had been delicious, but then, living alone, he had no doubt had to learn how to look after himself.

'We'd better get the socks, otherwise we're going to be late.' He walked over to the dresser and opened a drawer, and then turned to Holly, and said, 'I suspect it would save time if you got them out for me.'

Obligingly, Holly went to the open drawer. Because Drew had opened it to its fullest extent, there was hardly enough space between his body and the bed for her to get past, but she managed it by wriggling slightly.

'Here you are. I think these are black,' she told him breathlessly, rifling through the drawer until she found the right pair. 'I'll ... I'll wait for you outside while you put them on.'

She saw his eyebrows lift and blushed furiously, but he didn't make the kind of scathing comment Howard would have made in the same circumstances, simply smiling at her and watching her go.

She had forgotten that he was colour-blind, she mused as she waited for him; that would, of course, explain the awful combination of red sweater and brown cords into which he had changed last night.

Howard had perfect clothes sense. So perfect, in fact, that at times he criticised Holly's own choice. Take this dress she was wearing tonight, for instance. Howard didn't like her wearing red, he preferred her in pastel colours; he considered them to be far more feminine.

Drew didn't keep her waiting long, ushering her outside into the cool October evening.

She was about to cross the yard when he forestalled her, swinging her up into his arms as he had done the previous day.

'Drew!' she protested breathlessly.

'You're wearing those idiotic heels again,' he growled. 'Don't you ever wear sensible shoes?'

'I can't,' she told him sadly. 'I'm only five foot two, you know. I need the height.'

'What for?'

For some reason his question flustered her, and she was glad that they had reached the Land Rover. Or had they? She peered at the vehicle in front of them, realising that it wasn't the one she had travelled in the previous day.

'Drew, this is a Range Rover.'

'So it is,' he agreed laconically.

It was almost brand new as well, Holly recognised as she saw the number-plate, and so luxurious inside that her eyes rounded in surprise.

'I didn't know you owned this.'

'No? Well, you wouldn't, would you?'

'But, Drew, they're terribly expensive.'

She couldn't help remembering how as a teenager Drew had always had less money than the rest of them, and she suspected he must have bought the vehicle in a last-ditch attempt to impress Rosamund.

Poor Drew, she thought, tears stinging her eyes as he got in beside her and started the engine. His situation was so much worse than hers. At least she could

escape back to London, but Drew would be forced to
live almost side by side with Rosamund and Howard.
But at least that way he would be there as a constant
reminder of what they had once shared, while
Howard . . .

They drove through the village and out again along
the road off which Rosamund's father had built his
house. The last time Holly had visited it had been for
Rosamund's eighteenth birthday. That had been one
May, with a marquee on the lawn and every other
fashionable expense Rosamund's mother could think
of.

Tonight there was no marquee, but the line-up of
cars down the long drive was evidence of the new
social sphere in which Rosamund and her parents
moved—Porsche, Jaguar, Mercedes and Rolls—and
a tiny tremor of fear quaked through Holly.

Drew found a parking spot half-way down the drive,
parking the Range Rover with commendable expertise.

Someone was walking down the drive toward them;
a couple, to judge from the light female voice and its
deeper male counterpart.

The footsteps stopped as they drew level with the
Range Rover, and a voice Holly vaguely recognised
demanded, 'Drew, is that you?'

'Hello, Jane—and Guy. How are you?'

'Oh, we're fine.'

Of course, Jane Phillips; Holly remembered her
now. She had been quite a few years ahead of her in
school. In the same class as Drew, come to think of
it.

'Good heavens!' she exclaimed as Holly stepped
forward. 'It's Holly Witchell, isn't it? Well, now, how

long have you two been together? Guy and I have just come back from the States. Guy's been working over there for six months. Is this a new thing, or...?'

'Stop gossiping, woman, I'm freezing,' her husband interrupted.

When Drew would have fallen into step beside him Holly tugged on his arm and fibbed, 'Drew, I've left my handbag in the Range Rover.'

While Drew patiently unlocked the door, Holly waited until the other couple were out of sight and then hissed, 'It's all right, Drew. I've got my handbag here, but I've just had the most marvellous idea! Well, it was Jane who gave it to me, really.' She took a deep breath and then demanded, 'Why don't we pretend that we're in love?'

Drew went so still and silent that Holly wondered if she ought to have broken the idea to him more gently.

'With each other, I presume you mean?' he said cautiously at last.

'Yes, that's *exactly* what I mean,' Holly agreed, trying to control her impatience. Really, men could be so slow at times! Why on earth hadn't she thought of it before? It was the ideal way for both of them to reconjure their ex-partners' interest.

'But I thought you were in love with Howard?'

'I am,' Holly agreed. 'But can't you see, the moment he starts to think I've fallen in love with *you*, he's going to be so jealous... and of course, it will work the same way for you with Rosamund,' she added hastily, just in case he should accuse her of being selfish.

'Let me get this right,' Drew said slowly. 'You want us to pretend that *we're* in love?' He paused and then said slowly, 'How much in love, Holly? What I mean to say is, are we newly in love, or are we to be—er— established lovers?'

'Oh, newly in love, definitely,' Holly told him. 'You see, Howard is bound to guess what's going on other- wise. He only told me about Rosamund a couple of weeks ago.'

'Yes. Well, I can see that does rather complicate things. So, the impression we want to create is one of having taken one look at each other and fallen into one another's arms with cries of rapture.'

'Yes,' Holly agreed doubtfully, suddenly unable to imagine how on earth they were going to achieve such an implausible deception. 'You think it's a silly idea, don't you?' she said quietly. 'And I suppose you're right.'

'No, not silly,' he surprised her by saying unstead- ily, 'but maybe a trifle ambitious.'

In the light of the pseudo-Victorian streetlamps that illuminated the entire length of the drive in a fashion more suited to a motorway service station, Holly saw the smile he struggled to control. Strangely, she was not offended by it.

'I think we *could* perhaps carry it off, though, if we amended your plan slightly.'

Holly frowned and looked at him. 'How?'

'Well, let us suppose that we allow everyone to be- lieve that one of us—me, for instance—has been secretly, madly in love with you for years. You, having bumped into me, have suddenly realised how very fanciable I am, and here we are.'

'Well, yes,' Holly agreed doubtfully, 'but who's going to believe you've been secretly in love with me, when everyone knows you've been going out with Rosamund?'

'Well, it won't be easy. But think of the effect it will have on the happy couple. Rosamund is a very jealous woman. Once she hears that I've really been in love with you all these years . . . well, she won't like it.'

'No, I don't suppose she will,' Holly agreed faintly. She was beginning to feel almost jealous of Drew's inventiveness, wishing that *she* had been the one to get the role of the secretly pining lover.

'You know, it's a pity you have to rush back to London so soon,' Drew told her casually. 'I think if you could have managed to stick around for a while, the sight of us together would be almost bound to get results.'

'Yes,' Holly agreed regretfully. 'It's true what they say about propinquity.'

Drew muttered something under his breath, and she looked questioningly at him.

'Er—nothing. Is it agreed, then? When we arrive in the Jensens' drawing-room, we arrive as a couple?'

Holly took a deep breath and confirmed, 'Yes.'

And then, before she could change her mind, she took a deep breath and added, 'And I *could* stay on if you really think it might work, Drew. I've got over a month's worth of holiday owing to me. That's if you really think . . .'

'Oh, yes, I'm sure it will work,' he told her confidently. 'You could decorate the kitchen for me. I'd pay you, of course.'

'Oh, no!' Holly was horrified. 'Well, not unless you let me pay my board and food. Of course, I'll have to check with Jan, she's my boss, but I'm śure she won't mind. Things are relatively slack at the moment.'

'So it's settled. Right, then, are you ready to face your audience, Holly Witchell?'

'Yes . . . Yes, I think so.'

'Come on, then, let's go.'

CHAPTER THREE

'ANDREW! How lovely... Oh, and Polly, isn't it?'
Rosamund's mother said, in a voice far cooler than
the one she had welcomed Drew with.

'Holly, actually, Marsha,' Drew corrected her
calmly.

Somehow or other he had taken told of her hand,
Holly discovered, and he was now drawing her
forward, and tucking her against his side as though
she was as precious and delicate as rare porcelain.

It was a comforting feeling, having the warm bulk
of him there next to her; it gave her the confidence
to return Marsha Jensen's critical stare.

'What a very unusual dress,' the older woman
commented. 'Of course, we're rather out of touch with
London fashions.'

'Holly's wearing it especially for me. She knows I
love her in red.'

Holly was stunned. She stared at Drew, wondering
if she had heard him correctly. When had he got the
sophisticated confidence to pay such compliments,
and in such a lazily drawling voice that her arms had
come out in a rash of goose-bumps... or was that
because she could see Howard and Rosamund coming
toward them? Yes, of course it was.

'Drew, darling!' Rosamund cooed, leaving her new
fiancé's side to wrap thin white arms round Drew's

neck and to pull his head down so that she could kiss his mouth.

It was a very long kiss. A kiss which made Holly feel acutely uncomfortable and burningly angry on Drew's behalf. How dared Rosamund torment him like that, reminding him of what had once been?

Howard had no such embrace for *her*. He acknowledged her with a warm smile, though, his eyebrows lifting slightly as he studied her dress.

'*Red*, Holly?' he said teasingly. 'You know it isn't your colour.'

'On the contrary, I think it suits her,' Drew contradicted him flatly. 'And since she's wearing it for me, and not for you...'

'Good heavens, Drew darling, what on earth are you trying to say?' Rosamund interrupted with an acid look at Holly, but before Drew could say a word Jane and Guy joined them, Jane hugging Rosamund and congratulating Howard, and then stepping back to say excitedly, 'Rosamund, you've been keeping me in the dark. You wrote to tell me about you and Howard, but you never said a word about Drew and Holly.'

'Drew and Holly?'

The sharpness in Rosamund's voice made it carry, and several other people looked over to them, curious to know what was going on. Everyone went silent, and Holly felt as though the whole room was staring at them. Instinctively she nestled closer to Drew's side, welcoming the protective comfort of his arm around her.

To her relief, Drew broke the expectant silence, saying calmly, 'We weren't going to say anything yet.

We didn't want to spoil your thunder, did we, darling?'

Darling? Holly gulped and looked up at him, and for a moment was so dazzled by the look in his eyes that she could hardly even think, never mind articulate any thoughts.

'I see. So you'll be up here permanently from now on, will you, Holly?' Rosamund questioned coldly. 'Where will you be staying? Your parents' house still has tenants, doesn't it?'

'She's staying at the farm with me,' Drew announced quietly.

Now they really did have everyone's attention. A dark flush of unattractive colour stained Rosamund's face. Howard was staring at her as though he had never seen her before, Holly recognised, his eyes both accusing and angry.

'Good heavens, Holly,' Rosamund exclaimed brittlely, 'how very brave of you. I'm afraid I'm a little too old-fashioned for that kind of thing, and to be honest Mummy and Daddy would go spare if I even suggested it. Aren't you afraid that Drew will change his mind and refuse to marry you?'

To her own astonishment, Holly heard herself saying calmly, 'The days are gone when a woman needed to barter her virginity in exchange for the sometimes doubtful security of marriage, Rosamund. I think both Drew and I know what we're doing.'

She looked hesitantly at Drew, her eyes unconsciously pleading with him for help. He gave it promptly, dropping an unexpected kiss on her nose and saying, 'You're the one who's insisting on waiting. If I had my way I'd marry you tomorrow.'

He really was the most amazing actor, Holly mused, seeing the suddenly febrile glitter transform his eyes as he looked at her in a way that made unexpected tingles of sensation race up and down her spine.

Fortunately Rosamund's mother bustled them away before any further conversation could be exchanged. Once they were out of earshot of everyone else, Drew remarked cheerfully, 'Well, I think that certainly gave both of them something of a surprise.' And it was only then that Holly realised that she had been so absorbed in watching Drew that she hadn't even noticed how Rosamund and Howard had taken their announcement, other than to recognise their obvious shock.

'Something wrong?' Drew asked her solicitously, seeing her frown.

'No, not really.'

'How about making our way to the buffet, then? I'm starving.'

Half an hour later, sipping champagne and looking round for Drew, who had been waylaid by an older man Holly vaguely recognised as a partner in the local firm of accountants, she saw Jane walking towards her, smiling approvingly at her.

'I just came over to congratulate you both, and to tell you not to pay any attention to Rosamund's cattiness.'

'I suppose it's only natural that she should feel jealous.'

Jane gave her an odd look, and said hesitantly, 'Oh, you know about that, do you? I wasn't sure. Look, Guy and I are having a party later in the month to celebrate moving into our new house. We'd love both of you to come; perhaps I can even pick your brains a little. We haven't done anything about decorating it yet.' She pulled a face. 'There are quite a few interior design places in Chester, but I'm a bit frightened of being swamped by their ideas and the house not reflecting Guy's and my identity, if you know what I mean.'

'With a good designer, that won't happen,' Holly assured her. 'But I'll be only too pleased to advise you if I can. My speciality is decorative paint finishes, rather than the actual designing.'

It was true, but it was also true that Jan had told her she had a flair for the design side of things as well, and she had been encouraging Holly to develop that latent talent, generously sharing with her her own experience and knowledge.

'Girl talk?' Drew asked, coming over to join them. Odd how she hadn't realised how tense she was until she felt him standing behind her; the heat from his body warming hers and easing the tension out of her muscles.

Holly turned to smile at him. 'Not really. Jane was just inviting us to her housewarming party.'

'We wouldn't miss it...would we?' He reached out and caught hold of her hand, lifting it to his mouth and placing a warm kiss in the vulnerable hollow of her palm, making her tremble and stare at him with bemused eyes.

'Aha! Still at that stage, are you?' Jane laughed knowingly. 'Well, in that case, I'll leave you to it.'

'What was that for?' Holly asked huskily when she had gone. They were surrounded by other people, but she felt as though they were completely alone, isolated from the rest of the world, and she was protected from it by Drew himself.

'Rosamund and Howard were watching us,' he told her casually. 'I thought it was a good opportunity to further our cause.'

Feeling like a complete idiot, Holly blinked and looked away from him. *She* couldn't see Howard or Rosamund, had been totally oblivious to everything but the tingling sensation of the kiss Drew had placed against her skin.

'Has Neston said anything to you yet?' Drew asked her.

Holly shook her head. 'Has Rosamund said anything to you?'

'No.'

The band Rosamund's parents had hired for the evening had struck up a sentimental waltz, and Rosamund and Howard were dancing.

It was odd watching him dance with someone else, Holly reflected. He looked different somehow—smaller. Of course, Rosamund was much taller than she was, and compared with Drew, Howard looked... Well, he looked insignificant, she realised with a sudden shock.

It wasn't like watching someone she had loved for almost six years at all. It was like watching a stranger. A self-satisfied, selfish stranger who meant nothing to her at all.

The shock of that realisation made her tense, and Drew, standing beside her, was instantly aware of it. He took her hand in his and squeezed it reassuringly, and although he said nothing Holly felt tears burn her eyes.

Nice, kind Drew. How comforting it was to have him here at her side. Without knowing it she edged closer to him, unaware of the way he looked down at her, or of the glint in his eyes when he saw what Holly had not: that the newly engaged couple dancing together on the other side of the room seemed far more interested in them than in each other.

Other people started to dance, but Holly was relieved when Drew didn't suggest that they join them. Howard hated dancing with her, he claimed that she had two left feet, but then the band struck up a number which had soared into the pop charts, albeit quite some time ago, but which was instantly recognisable and obviously very popular, and Drew turned to her and said softly, 'We can't miss out on this one.'

It was 'Lady in Red', and somehow or other, as he drew her on to the dance-floor and the haunting sound of the music swelled round them, Holly found it incredibly easy to simply let Drew take her in his arms and keep her there while they moved in time to the music.

Her body seemed to move in time with his with a floating ease that required no effort or concentration. She was vaguely aware of Rosamund and Howard dancing past them, Rosamund glaring at her with angry eyes, Howard pursing his mouth. He had always had a rather thin mouth, she reflected, not like Drew's. She looked up at him to study it, and a tiny curl of sensation tensed her stomach.

The music ended far too soon. She could have danced with Drew all night, but they were already being summoned to drink a toast to the newly engaged couple, and it was then, seeing the diamond glittering on Rosamund's finger, hearing the speech given by her father, that reality crashed in through her barriers and she realised that the man she loved was now committed to someone else.

She turned away and would have left the room if Drew hadn't stopped her, gripping her arm and forcing her to remain.

The elation generated by their 'plan' had carried her through the evening so far, but now it had gone, leaving her feeling flat and drained and miserably aware of how little in terms of social and financial benefits her parents could have given Howard in comparison to Rosamund's. Hard on the heels of this knowledge was the shocking awareness of the fact that she must have known for a long time that Howard was materialistic, even if she had never admitted it to herself.

'Not much longer,' Drew said at her side, 'and then we'll be able to leave.'

Holly wanted to ask him if they could leave now, but she forced herself to give him a bright smile and say gaily, 'So soon? We've barely been here five minutes.'

He gave her a long, thoughtful look, and she found it odd that a man who really knew so little about her should be able to regard her with a penetrating intensity that told her there wasn't a thought in her head he wasn't aware of, while Howard, who had known her for so long, had often upset her by being totally unaware of what she was thinking or feeling. Was it because Drew cared about people, while Howard didn't?

She could not allow the traitorous thought room to grow, so she banished it, reminding herself that Howard's world was different from Drew's.

Rosamund's mother came up to talk to Drew, deliberately excluding Holly from the conversation. She wandered away from him, nursing her empty glass of champagne, feeling more alone and betrayed than she had ever imagined she could feel. What was she doing here, pretending to be in love with Drew?

'Holly! At last ... I've got to speak to you.'

Howard's sudden materialisation at her side made her jump. She had wandered into the conservatory, away from the noises of the band and the chatter of the other guests, lured there by the tranquillity and peace.

'What's going on?' Howard demanded abruptly. 'What's all this about you and Drew?'

'I think that's our business, don't you?' she managed to say, holding her head proudly.

'Oh, come off it; this time fourteen days ago you were telling me that you were desperately in love with *me*. You begged me not to get engaged to Rosamund.'

'Howard,' she protested tearfully, almost sagging with relief when Drew's familiar voice said from behind,

'I think you've said enough.'

'Enough? I haven't even started,' Howard said angrily. 'I don't know what game you two are playing ...'

'It's no game,' Drew told him softly, and to Holly's astonishment Howard was the first one to look away, angry colour burning his skin as Drew held his ground.

'I love Holly and she loves me, and that's all you or anyone else needs to know.'

'Holly?'

She took a deep breath and, looking not at him, but at Drew, as though just by looking at him she could draw strength and courage from him, she said shakily, 'What Drew says is true, Howard.'

'I've loved her for one hell of a long time,' Drew lied easily, staggering Holly with his *sang-froid*. 'And your loss is most definitely my gain. Only, unlike you, I'm never going to let her go. Come on, darling,' he said softly to Holly, 'it's time to go home.'

He led her firmly away without allowing Howard to say another word.

Holly was so bemused that she couldn't say a word until they were in the Range Rover and driving away from the ostentatious modern house.

'It's not going to work, Drew,' she said miserably. 'I should never have suggested it. Of course Howard will never believe I'm in love with you.'

She saw the way his fingers curled tensely on the steering wheel and looked up at him in surprise. Shadows masked his eyes, but she could see the tautness of his jaw. A small muscle flickered there, and a shaft of light showed her the surprising grimness of his expression.

'Then we'll just have to find a way to make him, won't we?' he said curtly.

She was on the verge of protesting mournfully that there wasn't much point, that seeing Howard with Rosamund had underlined all too clearly to her how little he had really cared about her—how little he was actually capable of caring about anyone other than himself, she thought honestly—and then she remembered that these weren't only her feelings and her future involved here. There were Drew's as well. Instantly contrite, she reached out and covered his hand with her own. So much smaller and frailer, for all that she was used to thinking of it as a very capable and sturdy hand, the nails cut short and neat to facilitate her work, but against Drew's it looked tiny and very feminine.

'I'm sorry,' she apologised huskily. 'I was being selfish. Rosamund couldn't take her eyes off us. I think our plan may work where she's concerned.'

'But not with Howard?' Drew questioned.

'I don't know,' Holly admitted honestly. 'Seeing him tonight . . .' She lifted her head and looked at him and admitted with painful honesty, 'Tonight it was as though I'd never really seen him before. He wants all the advantages that Rosamund's parents can give them. My parents . . .'

'And so you're resigned to losing him?'

'I don't know,' she admitted in a troubled voice. 'I don't know what to think any more.'

And the root cause of her confusion wasn't so much Howard, but Drew, she recognised helplessly. For some reason, being with Drew had thrown into sharp relief facets of Howard's personality she had never really acknowledged before—unpleasant and unwanted facets.

'Are you saying that you've changed your mind?' Drew asked carefully. 'That you no longer want to go through with our plan?'

She was tempted, but they had made an agreement, and for Drew's sake they *should* go on with it.

Rosamund had been jealous, Holly acknowledged. She had seen it in the other girl's eyes on more than one occasion.

'No, not that. Unless you've changed your mind?'

'No... No, I haven't done that,' Drew told her, and she could almost feel the release of tension from his body. Had he been afraid that she *would* change her mind, that she would back out of their agreement? He must love Rosamund very much, she acknowledged, not knowing why she should find the knowledge so dispiriting. A wave of tiredness engulfed her. It had been a long day, and now all she wanted to do was to sleep. She stifled a yawn and Drew chuckled.

'You look about sixteen when you do that,' he told her.

Immediately she flushed. She knew she looked young for her age, that she did not possess the sophisticated gloss of a woman like Rosamund. Howard had often urged her to buy clothes that made her look older, and she had always stoutly defended her right to wear what she felt comfortable in, but all at once she felt very vulnerable and immature.

'I was thinking,' Drew told her as he turned the Range Rover into the farmyard, 'it isn't just my home that could do with revamping, with a woman's touch. It's me, as well.'

Holly stared at him, and saw a thin tinge of red darken his skin. He was embarrassed about asking for her help. Immediately her heart went out to him.

'You look fine in what you're wearing tonight,' she assured him.

'Yes, but if it hadn't been for you I'd have gone out in green socks,' he pointed out to her humorously. 'Do you think you could take me in hand a little, Holly? Turn me into the sort of man who would appeal to a woman?'

Holly didn't know what to say. She wanted to reassure him that he already had all the qualities any woman of sense could want, but to do so would be to insult Rosamund, and it was *her* that he loved.

The Rosamunds of this world liked men as strikingly socially confident as they were themselves. Men like Howard, who spent a fortune on their clothes and enjoyed dressing the part they had cast for themselves. Not men like Drew, who cheerfully wore ancient jeans and old shirts.

'You mean, help you choose new clothes?' she asked hesitantly.

'Yes, that sort of thing. Give me a few tips on the kind of things women like in a man.'

'It will be expensive,' she told him shyly, nibbling on her bottom lip, and adding, 'I know that things haven't been easy for you, Drew. Moneywise, I mean.'

To her amusement, he laughed. 'Times change, Holly. I think I can afford to buy a few new clothes. When shall we start? I've got a free afternoon on Monday. We could go to Chester.'

'That sounds fine. I'll have to check with Jan, though, first, and make sure I can have the time off. Drew, do you mind that people will think...well, that we're lovers?' she asked hesitantly.

'Do you?' he countered abruptly.

She shook her head, surprised to discover that it was true.

'It could get back to your parents' ears,' he warned her.

'They'll understand when I explain to them.' She stifled another yawn.

'Come on,' Drew told her. 'It's time you were in bed.'

'You must be tired too...'

'Yes,' he agreed bleakly, and, watching the expression darken his eyes, Holly felt her heart contract with pity for him. This must be so much worse for him than it was for her. Men had their pride, after all; and he would have to go on living here in the same vicinity as Howard and Rosamund, while she could escape back to London and her job.

She caught herself up. What *was* she thinking? The whole purpose of her staying here, of their plan, was to make sure that Howard and Rosamund didn't marry.

Holly woke up on Sunday morning with a horrid feeling of foreboding. And then she remembered the engagement party!

She sat up bolt upright in bed. She must have been mad to suggest to Drew that they pretend to have fallen in love in order to make Rosamund and Howard jealous. And Howard hadn't even believed her!

It said a great deal for how desperately in love with Rosamund Drew must be to even have considered going along with her suggestion, never mind carrying it out with such aplomb. Far more aplomb, in fact, than she had ever visualised.

Rosamund *had* been jealous. There had been no doubt about that. Well, she had never liked Holly, even when they were at school together. She had come from the wealthiest family in the village, and yet Holly could vividly remember one Christmas being given a much-coveted set of oil paints. Only six of them, because they were very expensive, but within a week Rosamund, who barely knew one end of a paintbrush from another, had arrived at school with twice as many paints as Holly and she had lost no time in showing them off to her small coterie of friends. As a girl she had never been able to endure someone having something she did not, and it seemed that she hadn't changed—right down to resenting someone being with her cast-off boyfriend. But would her jealousy be sufficient to make her turn from Howard back to Drew?

He must want her back desperately indeed if he was prepared to solicit her own help in revamping his image, Holly reflected.

The thought made her feel unaccountably depressed, and she was still sitting up in bed dwelling on it when Drew knocked on her door and called out cheerily, 'I hope you're awake now, sleepyhead.'

He had walked in before Holly could ask him not to, and as she dived for the protection of the bedclothes she saw him looking very amused.

'What's wrong?' he demanded, his grin widening as he studied her indignant expression. 'Don't tell me you sleep in the nude?'

She didn't, and common sense told her that there was nothing remotely revealing about her serviceable cotton nightshirt, and that her modesty was both unnecessary and idiotic, but for some reason it touched a tiny sore place within her that Drew should find it unlikely that she was the kind of sensuously aware woman who enjoyed the eroticism of sleeping with her body bare.

'I've brought you a cup of coffee,' he added, walking over to the bed and sitting on the edge of it, putting the mug on the bedside-table. 'Sleep all right?' he queried. 'You were certainly dead to the world when I looked in on you earlier.'

'Earlier!' Holly looked at her watch and protested, 'It's only just gone nine now. What time did you get up?'

'Six,' Drew told her wryly. 'Sunday is the cow-man's day off, and I do the milking. Not that we keep a large dairy herd these days. Fortunately I could see where things were heading with the milk quotas, and I switched over to beef and breeding at the right time.'

Forgetting her undressed state, Holly sat up, drawing her knees up to her chest and hugging her arms round them, asking eagerly, 'What made you do that? Cheshire has always been a milk-producing county...'

'Oh, this and that. A bit of listening and a lot of reading, and a small helping of intuition.'

'And that's why you have the bull. For stock breeding.'

'Yes. I'll show you some of his offspring later. That is... if you're going to stay.'

'Well, I'll have to check with Jan.' She bent her head, so that her hair swung forward, concealing her voice, her voice slightly muffled as she said hesitantly, 'Drew, what I said last night about making Rosamund and Howard jealous... do you really think it can work?'

He was quiet for so long that she thought he wasn't going to reply, so the sudden shock of his fingers, brushing her hair back off her face and tilting her chin so that he could look at her, caught her off guard.

She wasn't used to being touched, she recognised, as her heart started to thud and her nerve-endings relayed to her brain the pleasurable sensation of having Drew's work-roughened fingers lightly touching the softness of her skin. Howard had never touched her unless it was a prelude to kissing her, and over these last months there hadn't even been that . . . just a very few brief, dry kisses, given on his arrival and departure. She, fool that she was, had never even had the wit to recognise his dying sexual interest in her for what it was.

Not, now that she came to think of it, that he had ever evinced much desire for her at all. Her throat suddenly dry, she asked impulsively, 'Drew, if you loved someone, and they didn't want to make love, what would you do?'

It had suddenly struck her that there was something very ominous about the fact that Howard had never once suggested a more intimate physical relationship.

Even with her lashes lowered, she could feel the penetrating heat of Drew's gaze.

'Well,' he said evenly, 'that would depend. First I'd want to know why she was reluctant to make love. If it was because she didn't desire me, then I think I'd admit defeat and the relationship would end. However, if I thought it was because she was inexperienced, or uncertain—why, then I think I'd probably try to show her that there was nothing to fear.'

'You wouldn't just...not do anything, then?' Holly asked him.

'I shouldn't think so. Do you still want me to answer your first question?'

A strange tension seemed to have filled the room, but his prosaic words banished it. Holly drew a faintly shaky breath. Why was it that every word Drew said only seemed to confirm her own growing fear that Howard had never really loved her at all?

He must have read something of what she was thinking in her face because he released her abruptly and said tersely, 'Neston must be mad. Don't give up, Holly.'

'No. No, I won't,' she agreed. 'After all, they aren't married yet, are they? Oh, Drew, you're encouraging me to be selfish,' she exclaimed remorsefully when he went quiet. 'Here I am moaning on about *my* feelings, and it's just as bad for you. You must have hated seeing them together last night.'

'It's always painful loving someone who loves someone else,' he agreed. He got up off the bed. 'I've got a few things to do. Why don't you get up, make that phone call to your boss, and then I'll take you out somewhere for lunch?'

'I thought farmers were far too busy to go out for lunch.'

'Normally we are, but we managed to get the harvest in early, and the autumn ploughing is well under way. Where do you fancy going? They've done up a couple of the local pubs and they serve pretty good lunches, or we could go into Chester and try for

the Grosvenor. I'd take you to Rookery Hall, but we'd
need to book well in advance.'

'A pub sounds just fine,' Holly told him. 'Or if you
like we could stay here. You don't have to entertain
me, Drew. After all, I have rather inflicted myself on
you.'

To her astonishment he leaned down and kissed her
lightly on her mouth.

'What was that for?' she asked him.

'Just for being you,' he told her, tugging gently on
her hair.

He had kissed her as he might have done a favourite
young cousin, she reflected after he had gone, and
she couldn't quite help wondering how he kissed Rosamund. She suspected that well-shaped mouth could
do devastating things to a woman's self-control, and
then wondered a little sadly why it was that no man
ever seemed remotely tempted to kiss her with the
passion she had once naïvely assumed she would share
with Howard, once they were married.

CHAPTER FOUR

HOLLY rang Jan from Drew's office, a comfortable, shabby room which was down a passage that led into the yard.

'Hang on a minute,' Jan demanded, when she had given her a breathless account of all that had happened. 'I've only been up for half an hour, Holly, and I'm not quite capable of grasping all that lot in one go. Explain properly.'

And so she did, hesitating a little as she got to the point where she had suggested to Drew that they pretend to be lovers.

'And he agreed?' Jan said doubtfully.

'Well, he's desperately in love with Rosamund,' Holly told her quickly. 'He wants me to stay on, Jan. And I'd like to. I've got plenty of holidays due to me. He's even got a commission for me.'

She went on to explain to Jan about the kitchen.

'Well, I must admit all this rather ties in with something Luke and I were discussing the other night. I'm thinking—only thinking, mind—of starting up an outlet in the north, Holly, and what I have in mind is for you to take charge of it for me. It would involve a lot of work. You'd have to canvass around to find the right spot, and then there'd be discussions with the bank and our accountants. If you like, while you *are* going to spend some time up there, you could start looking around, get a feel for the market. Of course, we'd make you a partner in the business, and we'd talk about splitting the profits of the new outlet, but first I need to know if you're interested.'

'Interested? Jan, I'm stunned! I'm not a designer.'

'Maybe not, but you're very good with people, Holly, and the clients like you, which is important. They find you *simpatico* and they're not afraid to tell you what they want, which makes them come back, rather than simply smiling and saying it's wonderful, when in truth they hate what we've done. Look, don't make any decision right now. Have a think about it while you're up there. I can easily spare you for a month.' She hesitated and then warned doubtfully, 'Don't set too much store on this plan of yours, will you, love?'

'You mean, you don't think I'll get Howard back,' Holly interrupted her in a quiet voice.

'Oh, Holly, I *know* you *think* you love him, but believe me, you're better off without him. Tell me more about this Drew,' Jan pressed her curiously.

Holly did, and at such length that when Jan came off the telephone she was grinning to herself.

'What was that all about?' Luke demanded, coming into the room in time to catch the tail-end of the phone call and his wife's expression.

'Nothing much. Holly wants to take up her holiday allocation. I've had a word with her about the new outlet and asked her to have a canvass round.'

'And that makes you grin like a Cheshire cat?'

'No,' Jan told him, but refused to be drawn any further.

*   *   *

'Did you manage to get through to your boss?' Drew asked half an hour later, walking into the kitchen and bending to remove his muddy wellingtons.

'Yes. She's quite happy for me to stay. And guess what?'

Quickly she explained to him Jan's proposition, wondering why it was that she found it so much easier to talk to Drew than she ever had to Howard. Howard had found her job boring and had made no attempt to pretend otherwise, cutting her off when she talked about it so that he could instead talk about his own business life. Sometimes she had felt almost resentful because she enjoyed her work, and Howard's lack of interest in it detracted from her own sense of self-satisfaction in what she did.

Drew, on the other hand, seemed gratifyingly interested, even coming up with one or two suggestions as to where a good outlet might be.

'Chester is the obvious choice, but it's very pricey. There's Knutsford, of course—and then Nantwich.'

'Nantwich?'

'Mmm. I'll have to see if I can arrange some time off, and I'll drive you round, if you like.'

'Oh, Drew, would you?'

'Why not? After all, it will all help to reinforce the image, won't it?'

'The image?'

'Of the pair of us as inseparable lovers.'

'Oh, yes.' Holly was mortified to discover that in her excitement she had almost forgotten about that.

* * *

They were still talking about Jan's proposed new venture and Holly's role in it when they set out for lunch an hour later.

Holly was wearing a new skirt of tartan, with a toning sweater in the same dark blues and greens of the skirt, and over it an acid-yellow jacket which picked out the acid yellow line of the tartan.

It suited her, and had been an expensive buy, at least as far as she was concerned, and bought on impulse, even though she had known that Howard wouldn't like it.

Drew did, though, his complimentary praise bringing a happy glow to her cheeks.

Like her, he was casually dressed, but in a way that made her all too well aware of what he meant when he said that he needed a woman's advice and help.

There was nothing specially wrong with the beige cords, other than the fact that they didn't do justice to his physique; mainly, Holly suspected, because they had been designed for someone far more generously proportioned around the hips than Drew, and she wondered rather wistfully what he would look like in a pair of well-cut, stone-washed jeans.

As though the cords weren't bad enough, he had chosen to wear with them a garish checked shirt in red and green, and over it a blue sweater.

She thought of Howard's carefully chosen separates and immaculately tailored suits and made herself vow that, in appearance at least, Drew would be able to rival Howard before she was finished with him.

She would need more clothes herself in view of the length of her stay. Jan had a spare key for her flat and had promised to send some things on to her, but in the meantime it might be as well if she bought a new pair of jeans. She could wear them while she was working on Drew's kitchen.

She hadn't checked with him yet what kind of colour scheme he had in mind, and when she mentioned this he shrugged his shoulders and said indifferently, 'I'll leave that up to you.'

'But, Drew, presumably you designed the kitchen for Rosamund. Does she have a favourite colour?'

He took his attention off the road and looked at her. 'Baby pink,' he told her flatly, 'and if you dare to paint my kitchen that colour, I shall wring your neck.'

Holly could only agree with him, but she was surprised at his attitude. She had rather gained the impression that if Rosamund had wanted the kitchen painted all the colours of the rainbow, he would have been delighted to oblige her.

'Yellow would be pretty and fresh—with just a hint of blue...perhaps in the stencilling. Or I could simply lime the oak and leave it as it is. That would be more austere, but very effective.'

'Do something that you would like if it was your own kitchen,' Drew told her.

'But *you* might not like it,' she protested.

He turned his head and smiled at her. 'Just as long as it isn't baby pink, I'll like it,' he assured her.

The pub was obviously a popular venue for people to gather for either lunch or a drink. Jane and Guy were standing in the bar when Drew ushered her in. She liked the way he kept her close to his side, she reflected as she fell back, slightly awed by the busy press of people. It made her feel safe and protected. Jane waved to her, and called them over.

'Everyone's all agog over the news about you and Drew,' she told Holly cheerfully while Drew went to the bar. 'You've caused quite a bombshell. Oh, heavens, here's Rosamund and Howard. That's odd. Rosy doesn't normally come slumming here. Rookery Hall or the Grosvenor is more her scene. Are you two lunching?'

'Yes, we are,' Drew announced firmly, arriving with their drinks, 'and as we're a little bit late, I think we'd better go through.'

He started to usher Holly away almost immediately, and she wondered if he realised that he was missing an ideal opportunity to show Rosamund that he wasn't pining for her.

She tried to tell him as much, but the level of conversation around them was so high that by the time she had got her message across they were already in the dining-room.

A rather odd look crossed his face when she told him that Howard and Rosamund had arrived, and if Holly hadn't known better she could almost have thought that he was annoyed at their presence.

They were given an attractive table in the window, overlooking the fields to the rear of the pub.

Holly followed Drew's recommendation and ordered the traditional roast beef, and while she waited for their soup to arrive she kept looking anxiously toward the door.

'Stop looking so anxious,' Drew told her curtly. 'They won't come in here. Rosamund won't eat anything that isn't served raw and decorated with kiwi fruit.'

The dry way he said it made Holly look closely at him. His comment had almost been sarcastic, something she wouldn't have expected, given his feelings for Rosamund. He was probably just trying to pretend he wasn't affected by their break-up, she decided sympathetically.

The dining-room was busy, and the waiter came up to their table to explain in a flustered manner that there was no more home-made soup left.

'There's pâté, or a seafood mousse . . .'

'Either sounds delicious,' Holly assured him with a sunny smile, at pains to let him know that she understood that the absence of the soup wasn't his fault, and then she realised that Drew was watching her closely.

'What's wrong?' she asked him uncertainly, flushing a little. 'Have I got a smut on my nose?'

'No.'

'Then why are you looking at me like that?'

'I was just reflecting how very pleasant and relaxing it is to be with a woman who treats everyone around her with such consideration.'

Holly blushed a deeper pink at his praise; it gave her a warm glow deep inside, a happy feeling of well-being she hadn't experienced in a long, long time . . . and certainly not with Howard. At least, not recently.

'It's only a bowl of soup,' she told him honestly.

'Mmm . . . but I know women who'd have raised the roof, just for the pure hell of it.'

Women, or one woman? She could quite easily see Rosamund doing just that.

The waiter brought them the pâté, with another apologetic smile.

It was delicious and Holly told him as much when he came to collect their plates and serve the main course.

There was a warm, happy atmosphere in the cosy, low-beamed room; several tables were occupied by family groups, including children, all of whom were cheerfully well behaved.

This was what she missed in London, she acknowledged: this sense of belonging, of being part of a community.

'Don't think about him,' Drew advised her harshly.

She stared at him and suddenly realised what he meant.

'I wasn't,' she said honestly. 'I was thinking how much I've missed all this.'

'I've never really been able to see you as a city girl.'

'Needs must,' Holly said lightly. 'I needed a job——' she shrugged comprehensively '—but I must say I'm thrilled about Jan's suggestion.'

'She obviously thinks very highly of you. Tell me some more about your work.'

'Oh, no. It's your turn to tell me about yours,' Holly told him.

'There isn't much to tell. I left school at sixteen when my father died, as you know. It was hard going at first, but I was lucky enough to have the advice of a family friend. My stepfather now, actually. He encouraged me to take a night-school course. That opened my eyes to a great deal, showed me where my father had been going wrong.'

'So the farm's profitable now?' Holly asked him.

'Profitable enough to pay your fees,' he teased her.

Immediately Holly put down her knife and fork and said firmly, 'There won't *be* any fees, Drew—not unless you let me pay you board and lodging.'

'All right, firebrand, calm down. I'd forgotten how feisty you can be,' he added with a chuckle.

Feisty? Her? Privately, Holly always considered herself boringly calm and dull.

'Do you really see me as feisty, Drew?' she asked doubtfully.

'Does it matter how I see you? I thought Neston's opinion was the only one that counted.'

Suddenly he seemed to have withdrawn from her, and she shivered slightly, as though the sun had gone in, leaving her feeling exposed and cold. Oddly enough, his opinion *did* matter, although she could not for the world have said why. Perhaps it was because she knew instinctively that Drew would never lie, that his responses would always be honest, no matter what the cost to others or himself.

'Pudding?' he asked her.

She shook her head. 'After that lot, I'll hardly be able to move as it is.'

'Coffee, then, and a liqueur?'

'No liqueur, but coffee—yes, please.'

It came as a shock to discover that they were the last people left in the dining-room. Drew had been making her laugh with his wry stories of the mistakes he had made when he first took over the farm, and the waiters looked over in their direction several times when Holly's bubbling laughter rang out, giving her trim form admiring glances, to which she was oblivious but of which Drew took due note.

She had never realised before that Drew had such a good sense of humour, and was moreover able to laugh at himself and his own errors. It encouraged her to tell him some of her own tales of things that had gone wrong in her early days working for Jan.

It was sad that she had never shared this warm camaraderie with Howard, she reflected as she refused a final cup of coffee and waited for Drew to pay the bill.

But then, she was in love with Howard, while Drew... well, Drew was a friend, his sex an immaterial part of their relationship.

Or was it? Traitorously, she remembered the tiny tingle of sensation his touch had evoked within her, firmly dismissing it as she tried to concentrate instead on recalling the feelings that Howard aroused in her. Astoundingly, that special mixture of despair and delight she always connected with Howard eluded her. She knew she loved him. She had always loved him, but she couldn't conjure up the magical memory of how she felt when he was with her.

'Ready to leave?'

She smiled warmly at Drew, enjoying the courteous way he pulled back her chair for her and escorted her out of the room.

Howard thought such attentions old-fashioned and unnecessary. Women were equal to men these days and therefore quite capable of opening their own doors and so on. Sometimes Holly wondered if Howard was quite as approving of women's equality as he said.

She had noticed on more than one occasion that he could be sneeringly unkind about some of the older career women he came across in his work.

There were still a few cars in the car park, proof perhaps that the pub's opening and closing hours were slightly more elastic than those of its city brethren, Holly reflected, as they headed for the Range Rover.

It was a lovely afternoon, autumnal and rich with the colours and scents of the season.

A brand new Jaguar saloon was parked next to the Range Rover, and Holly's heart did a nosedive as she recognised Howard and Rosamund standing next to it. They had obviously been chatting with the couple who were just getting into a scarlet Porsche parked several yards away.

Of course, Rosamund would have wealthy friends, and Howard would like that, Holly thought miserably. He had always been far more impressed by wealth and position than she was herself.

She pinned a bright smile to her face as they approached the other couple. It hurt to see Howard—*her* Howard—with someone else. Especially a someone else who was wearing his ring, especially a someone else like Rosamund.

On Howard's face was that same half-sulky, half-defiant expression it had worn when he had told her the news about his engagement, and Drew for once seemed unaware of her distress, almost purposefully distancing himself from her, so that she shivered, missing the warmth and reassurance of him at her side.

As she drew level with the other couple, Rosamund turned her and gave her a taunting look, and then to Holly's anguish she turned round and slid her arms around Howard, pressing her body the length of his with open sexuality, kissing him in a way that made Holly's face burn, so intimate was it. She had never seen people kiss like that in public before, and, inside, her self-confidence and belief in her own sexuality shrivelled a little more. Howard had never kissed *her* like that.

As she turned away from the embracing couple she heard Rosamund's low, satisfied laughter. Her face burning, she climbed into the Range Rover without a word, but her feelings showed quite clearly in her eyes, dark with misery and anguish.

They drove several miles in silence, and then Drew said harshly, 'It was only a kiss, Holly, and staged more for our benefit than their mutual enjoyment.'

She ignored the latter part of his statement and turned her head so that she could look at him, her eyes showing her deep inner torment.

'Yes, but he's never kissed me like that. No one has,' she added in a low voice. Her head bent forward, her hair masking her face, and revealing the slender arch of her throat.

Drew made no comment. But then, what comment *could* he make? He could hardly claim that Howard had felt passion for her when she realised all too well now that he had not. His lack of desire to make love to her had not sprung from a mutual lack of a high sex drive, but from uninterest in her sexually. She could see it now.

When they got back to the farm, Drew announced that he had to go and check on the stock. Holly offered to go with him, but he shook his head, and so instead she went up to her room, and got out the sketch book she always carried with her, trying to concentrate on a colour scheme for the kitchen.

For once her mind wouldn't focus on her work. She went downstairs again and wandered around the kitchen, stroking the wooden units, enjoying the sensation of their smoothness beneath her fingertips.

They felt warm and hard...rather like Drew's face, only then she had been touching blood and bone and had been conscious of the pulse of life beneath the warmth of his flesh, of the very maleness of him in contrast to her own femininity.

When Drew came back in, she was staring into space, sitting motionless in front of the window. He gave her a brief, assessing look and then said quietly, 'Why don't I light a fire in the sitting-room, and we can spend the evening discussing where we should start our search for your new premises? I've got plenty of maps.'

'You mean, instead of discussing how we're going to break Howard and Rosamund's engagement,' Holly countered in a hard, bitter voice she barely recognised as her own. She turned to him her eyes flashing fire and resentment. 'You don't need to wrap me in cotton wool, Drew. I can see the truth for myself. Howard never felt for me what he feels for Rosamund. The whole thing was a stupid idea... I might as well go right back to London.'

'You can't,' Drew told her steadily. 'It's too late for that. You've made a commitment ... Not just to help me, but to help Jan as well.'

He was right. She couldn't behave like a spoilt child and announce that she wasn't going to stay because she had realised in the space of three or four awful seconds that Howard didn't desire her.

'You're not still brooding about that kiss, are you?' Drew asked her quietly.

She refused to look at him, and said in a muffled voice, 'Wouldn't you be? Oh, Drew, what's wrong with me?' she wailed, suddenly unable to control her misery any longer. 'What is it about me that makes me so undesirable?'

He put down the basket of logs he had brought in and walked over to her, his hands gentle on her shoulders as he turned her to face him.

'Oh, Holly, you aren't undesirable,' he told her firmly. 'Far from it. Shall I prove it to you?' he asked her in a different voice, a voice free of any hint of amusement or mockery, but laced instead with a soft suggestion of sensuality that made her look disbelievingly at him.

Her mouth trembled slightly and Drew reached out and touched it with the hard pad of his thumb, drawing it over the softness of her bottom lip. A curious sensation shot through her, her body suddenly so weak that she was glad of the protective strength of Drew's arm when he pulled her gently against his own body.

He had discarded his jacket and she could feel the hardness of his muscles beneath the thinness of his shirt. His heartbeat was steady and reassuring; the clean, cold scent of fresh air clung to him, and, even as she recognised the peculiarity of being held like this by him when she was in love with someone else, her lips were parting moistly in obedience to the teasing pressure of his thumb. It rubbed gently against the edge of her teeth, and she had to suppress a sudden urge to nibble at the hard pad of flesh.

A forlorn awareness of how kind he was being in trying to reassure her swept over her, and she tried to protest to him that it was unnecessary, and that anyway she already knew that he did not desire her, but the words were never said because his mouth was touching hers.

She made a soft protest which made him tighten the firm hold of his arm so that she could feel the buckle of his belt digging into her, and the hand which had caressed her lips cupped her jaw, its fingers sliding into her hair, caressing the vulnerable flesh below her ear, and making her shudder discernibly, and press herself deeper into his embrace.

Deep in his throat, Drew made a soft, growling sound of satisfaction that brought her skin out in goose-bumps, and his lips, which had until then only been gently persuasive on her own, hardened and demanded in a way that made her forget everything bar the exciting sensations he was arousing in her.

Howard had never kissed her like this; never nibbled tormentingly at her lips; never teased their moist softness with his tongue; never held her or touched her as though she was infinitely desirable and precious.

She felt the increased thud of Drew's heart, and her own picked up the fierce beat; she felt his hand on her throat and parted her lips in obedience to the demands of his mouth.

'Open your eyes,' Drew whispered, and dazedly she did so, shocked to see the hot, dark colour burning his cheekbones, and the aroused glitter of his eyes.

'See what you do to me,' he whispered against her mouth. 'See how you make me feel, Holly.'

And before she could stop him, his hand slid down her spine, arching her into the hollow of his thighs so that she could feel his body's physical arousal.

Holly trembled, too shocked to do anything other than simply lean against him, the reality of his desire turning her so weak that she couldn't move.

This wasn't right. Drew didn't love her, nor she him…but he made her feel alive and feminine, needed in a way that Howard had never made her feel, her confused mind admitted.

She looked at him, his face so close to hers that she could see quite clearly the darker band of gold around each iris, and the thick black fan of his eyelashes, so long that she ached to reach out and touch them.

'Drew,' she protested shakily, her eyes clouding with tears of shock and fear. What was happening to her? It was wrong that she should feel like this, wrong that Drew should arouse her to desire without them sharing love. She had always believed that she would only feel desire where she felt love, and now, within the space of a few seconds, Drew had shown her how different reality was.

'I want you, Holly, and I could quite easily make you want me, too.'

'No!' She tensed in protest.

'Yes,' Drew told her grimly and, before she could stop him, his hand swept up over her body to cup her breast, his thumb unerringly finding the hard, tight pinnacle that betrayed the truth.

She drew in a sobbing breath of panic and distress, and begged huskily, 'Drew, please don't. It isn't right ... We don't—we don't love one another.'

'No,' he agreed, slowly releasing her, his eyes shadowed from her by the thick sweep of his lashes, his voice harsh and faintly biting, 'No, maybe not, but never let me hear you saying that you aren't desirable again, Holly, because it just isn't true.'

'But *Howard* doesn't desire me,' she protested miserably, and caught her breath on a stunned gasp as she saw the almost savage anger darken his face.

'And Neston is, of course, the only man of any importance in the entire male world!'

The biting sarcasm of the comment caught her off guard. She wasn't used to such sarcasm from Drew, and she stepped back from him uncertainly.

'I'm sorry, Holly,' he apologised, instantly contrite, and guiltily she recognised that this whole thing was as difficult for him as it was for her. More so, because he must surely have experienced a very full sex-life with Rosamund. So full, perhaps, that it was his frustration and longing for her that had caused his apparent desire for herself. She smiled wanly.

'I know you were only trying to help,' she said quietly. 'I'm sorry I'm being so stupid. If you'd like me to leave ...'

For a moment she thought he was going to agree. An odd look of despair combined with grimness crossed his face, but he mastered it and turned to her with a calm smile, 'Without decorating my kitchen? Come on, Holly, remember faint heart ...'

'Never won fair maid. Yes, I know. I suppose it is too soon to give up hope yet,' she agreed, but what she didn't tell him was that she was only just beginning to realise that the Howard she loved—that the Howard she *thought* she had known—was now proving to be little more than a creation of her own daydreams.

CHAPTER FIVE

'OH, NOT too bad,' Holly responded in guarded response to Jan's query as to how things were progressing.

Having discovered that it was virtually impossible locally to buy the paints and brushes she needed for her work, she had telephoned her boss to ask her to send on what she required.

'Drew is taking me out later. We're going to Chester today and then we'll do Nantwich and Knutsford another time.'

She didn't add that there was a dual purpose to their visit to Chester; namely, the refurbishment of Drew's wardrobe.

'Well, I've been round to your flat and packed what I think you'll need. I'm sending everything on by carrier, and it should be with you first thing tomorrow. I'll get the paints and brushes to you as quickly as I can. What colour are you doing the kitchen?'

'Yellow, I think, with touches of blue and white. It only has a small window, so that will look cheerful and bright. Oh, and while we're in Chester, Drew wants me to help him to revamp his wardrobe,' she added casually, adding in a conspiratorial whisper, 'He can't help comparing himself with Howard, and of course being colour-blind doesn't help.'

'Doesn't help what?' Jan demanded.

'Well, the way he looks. He wears all the wrong colours together, and his clothes never seem to fit him properly.'

'Oh, I see—you're going to give him a new image. Well, good luck. Whenever I take Luke shopping we end up having the most terrible row,' Jan told her forthrightly.

'Ready?' Drew asked, walking into the kitchen.

'Almost,' Holly told him, covering the receiver, and then saying a hasty goodbye to Jan.

They set off half an hour later. As Drew drove them toward the city, Holly brought up a problem which had been exercising her mind a great deal.

'It's all very well us deciding to make Howard and Rosamund jealous,' she announced, 'but how are we going to do that when they never see us together?'

'I thought perhaps that might be what you wanted . . . after Sunday,' Drew told her shrewdly.

For no reason at all, Holly felt herself growing hot and flustered as she remembered how Drew had kissed her, and how she had felt. He had simply been being kind to her, that was all. It was hardly his fault that things had well got a little out of control.

'Well, I was upset, seeing them together like that,' she admitted, and then rallied to add firmly, 'But I'm just going to have to get used to it.'

'You still think our plan will work, then?' Drew asked her.

Poor Drew. She tended to forget sometimes that she wasn't the only one suffering from a broken heart.

'Drew, I know it will,' she told him softly, reaching out to touch his arm.

It felt strong and hard beneath her fingertips, the sensation of the soft wool of his shirt moving against the warm skin, an oddly intimate experience. It made her feel peculiar inside, sort of aching and hot.

'But they've got to see us together,' she told him, quickly withdrawing her hand. 'We mustn't get disheartened.'

For some reason it had become very important that she kept the main purpose of her stay to the forefront of her mind. Sometimes, for some unaccountable reason it seemed in great danger of slipping slightly to the background and being overwhelmed by the pleasure she took in Drew's company, in her plans for the new business, in their discussions about both the past and the future, but more and more frequently about the future.

'Well, there's a local drama society's autumn play coming up soon. We could go to that.'

'Do you think they'll be there?' Holly asked eagerly.

Drew glanced at her. 'Rosamund's father is one of the sponsors. And then there's the "do" at the Grosvenor for Hallowe'en. Some sort of fancy-dress affair.'

'It doesn't sound Howard's cup of tea,' Holly said doubtfully. Howard hated dressing up; in fact, he hated anything that might in any way make him look even slightly foolish.

'It is at the Grosvenor,' Drew reminded her. 'There's also Lady Constance, the Countess of Telford's birthday party.'

'Of course. They're bound to be at that,' Holly agreed, brightening. The countess lived in a crumbling Tudor mansion several miles outside the village.

She was notoriously eccentric, and had been a widow for as long as Holly could remember. Every year she gave a birthday party to which the entire adult population of the village were invited, with one stipulation, and that was that the ladies of the village provided the food and the men the drink.

The birthday party was an institution, and there was no way that Rosamund or her parents would miss it. For one thing, Lady Constance always demanded the presence of her aristocratic relations, and Rosamund's parents would never dream of missing the opportunity to rub shoulders with the county élite.

They were in Chester now, Drew deftly parking the Range Rover in a convenient place.

'I had intended to take you to the Grosvenor for lunch, but my mother rang this morning, and once she knew you were home she insisted on inviting us to eat with them.'

Holly had forgotten that Drew had told her that his mother had moved to Chester on her remarriage.

'James, her husband, will be there. He only works part-time now. He set up his own financial consultancy when he left the bank.'

'Do you like him?' Holly asked him as she waited for Drew to lock the car.

'Very much. My father became very embittered during the last years of his life. He resented being left the farm in a way, and that resentment spilled over into all our lives. My mother was very loyal to him and I do believe that they loved one another, but James has made her happy in a way that I suspect my father never did.'

'And the others—your sister and the boys, do they like him?'

'Yes. And so they should! He's financing John through med. school at the moment and Paul at Oxford. Lucy's in Canada working for a newspaper group over there.'

Something in his voice made Holly ask quietly, 'Do you ever wish that you hadn't been the eldest?'

He looked at her as though her perception surprised him.

'Not often now, although I admit there was a time when I yearned to travel the world. Farming's in my blood, though, and it was James who taught me that being a farmer, being tied to the land, doesn't necessarily mean that a man's brain has to atrophy. There are other ways of travelling, ways that don't necessitate a journey further than the nearest library or paper shop,' he elucidated. 'Mind you, I suspect that if James hadn't encouraged me to go to night-school, and then helped me through the estate management course, I would have been in danger of following all my father's mistakes and making more of my own. Everything in life can be an adventure and a challenge if you let it.'

'Oh, I agree,' Holly told him fervently, remembering how disappointed she had been initially when she learned during her first year at art school that she just did not have the talent to become the artist she had dreamed of becoming.

It had been a bitter pill to swallow, and for a long time she had gone around in a cloud of despondency. That had been when Howard was taking a sabbatical following the completion of his own university course.

He hadn't been there when she needed him, she recollected wryly, and then chided herself for the disloyalty of her thoughts. It was hardly Howard's fault that she had discovered she would never make the grade as a painter when he wasn't there to comfort her.

'What's wrong?' Drew asked her, and she told him briefly, not mentioning her memories of Howard's absence.

'But in the end it all turned out for the best, because my tutor was so honest with me, he was able to direct me into other avenues, and I changed courses before it was too late—luckily for me. At the time I never imagined how much pleasure I would eventually get out of my work, especially when I'm asked to do murals.'

She went on to tell Drew about one commission she had received to copy a famous seventeenth-century allegorical ceiling from one of the great houses, but to give the cupids and cherubs the faces of various members of the family and friends. This ceiling, she added with a giggle, was in the bathroom.

'I expect it gave visitors quite a shock to look up and see their own features staring back at them. 'Oh, look!' she exclaimed. 'That looks like the kind of shop we need.'

They were almost opposite the window of a Jaeger shop selling classic men's separates. 'Do you want to go in?'

An exhausting two and a half hours later, Holly thought they had got a very good basis for Drew's new wardrobe. She particularly liked the chunky, soft tweed blouson jacket they had chosen, although Drew had demurred slightly about wearing the toning plain cashmere scarf with it.

The blouson was very dark charcoal grey with a fleck of pale and mid-blue, as well as off-white and rust. They had bought plain shirts in rust and blue to go with it, as well as a pair of trousers in plain matching charcoal.

There had been a few minutes' hiatus while Holly persuaded Drew that he had to have a couple of pairs of new jeans, especially when he discovered exactly what she had in mind. He had gone into the changing room and then emerged a good ten minutes later saying that the jeans were too fashionable for a country farmer, but nevertheless they were added to the growing pile of purchases.

Shoes, socks and ties to match the shirts, but in deep tones, a couple of sweaters, and then at the last minute, as they were leaving the shop, Holly turned to Drew and whispered urgently, 'Drew, what about underwear?'

And he dutifully disappeared back into the dark recess of the shop, to emerge a few minutes later clutching yet another carrier bag.

Holly would have liked him to have kept on the blouson jacket and the matching trousers, but he had refused, saying that he needed time to feel comfortable in them before he could wear them in public.

To the salesman's credit, he hadn't batted an eyelid at the awful combination of colours he had chosen to wear, which was more than could be said for his mother when she answered the door to them half an hour later.

Drew's mother and stepfather had a pretty house just outside the city centre, in a Regency terrace of soft red brick, with a long back garden that was completely walled.

'Come on in, both of you. Lunch is almost ready... You must be exhausted,' she added to Holly, when she had criticised her son on his choice of clothes and learned how they had spent their morning.

'You told me that you were bringing Holly to Chester so that she could look for possible premises,' she told her son severely, leading the way down a narrow hall and into a small, sunny dining-room. 'James will be down in a minute,' she told them as she offered them a pre-lunch sherry. 'Holly, you haven't changed at all, other than to grow even prettier,' she added with another smile. 'How are your parents? Still in New Zealand?'

'Yes. They've decided to live there permanently,' Holly told her.

She remembered Drew's mother as being a rather silent, harassed woman and she had been surprised to be greeted by this elegant, grey-haired fashion-plate with an almost model-girl figure, and a teasing, mischevious smile, especially when she looked at her oldest son.

'So you're staying with Drew.'

'Well, I had booked in at the Dog and Duck, but my car broke down.'

'And is still in Murphy's garage, awaiting a new tyre,' Drew chimed in, 'but it should be ready soon.'

'Drew's been very kind, taking me in,' Holly said awkwardly, not sure how much, if anything, Drew's mother knew about their plans.

Above her downbent head, mother and son exchanged a long look, and then Drew said easily, 'Well, all the kindness isn't on my side. Holly's going to paint the kitchen for me, and she's also revamped my wardrobe.'

'Not before time,' his mother agreed. 'Honestly, Drew, where on earth do you get your clothes? Ah, here's James,' she announced, getting up as her husband walked into the room.

James Talbot was a tall, spare man with grey hair and shrewd eyes. He shook Holly's hand firmly, and smiled at her. 'Drew tells me that you're interested in setting up a business locally,' he commented when they were all sitting round the table, eating Drew's mother's excellent lunch.

'Yes. Well, yes . . . although I'd only be involved as a very junior partner.'

She went on to explain Jan's business methods and expertise, until Drew cut in quietly, 'What she isn't telling you is that Holly herself is extremely well thought of by her employers. So well thought of, in fact, that they'd be wanting her to take full control.'

It was an odd sensation being part of a family group again, and listening to their warm and genuine praise. Holly missed her parents and her brother, but she was sensible enough to realise that it served no purpose to dwell on how alone she sometimes felt. But being with Drew and his family brought a painful lump of nostalgia to her throat, making it difficult for her to do anything more than shake her head in Drew's mother's enthusiastic approval of Jan's plans.

'And of course it would be so lovely for you to be home again. You know, Holly, you've never struck me as a city girl at all,' she added, unwittingly echoing Drew's own remarks.

'I don't think I am,' she agreed, and then her eyes clouded because, if she did succeed in getting Howard back, it would mean a return to London and the life they lived there, for she was quite sure that Rosamund's father would not allow him to remain in his prestigious job if he was no longer engaged to Rosamund.

Over coffee, Drew and his stepfather discussed investments and the financial aspects of farming, while Drew's mother brought Holly up to date on the lives of her other offspring.

There was a seven-year gap between Drew and his sister, and then another year between her and the twins, but Holly had only known them casually. However she was genuinely interested in their lives, even if occasionally she did find her concentration wandering to Drew and James.

'Drew has rather a flair for the stock market,' Louise told her, obviously aware of Holly's momentary lack of concentration. 'James believes he could have had a good future in it if he hadn't been so determined to farm.' She sighed faintly. 'I felt so guilty when Drew had to leave school after his father died, but he assures me that if he had his time all over again, he wouldn't change anything. A mother shouldn't have favourites, but I've always been that little bit closer to Drew than the others, perhaps because he was older at the time of his father's death. Don't hurt him, will you, Holly?' she asked quietly.

Don't hurt him? What kind of relationship did Drew's mother imagine they had?

'Drew tells me he's suggested Nantwich as a possible venue for your new business,' James announced, breaking into their conversation. 'It's a good choice. I'll tell you what, why don't the four of us go on Sunday? We could have lunch at Rookery Hall.'

Holly knew about the prestigious restaurant which had opened in the Victorian mansion just outside the town, but she hesitated before agreeing, looking questioningly at Drew. 'What about the stock?'

'I can get Tom to come in if I pay him overtime,' he assured her.

'Well, why don't we meet at around eleven? We can show Holly the town and then have lunch.'

'You won't recognise it,' Drew's mother told her. 'One or two very good dress shops have opened there, and the most wonderful place selling leather shoes and bags. They are out of this world . . . Italian mainly, I think.'

'Mmm. Just as well we're going on Sunday,' James said drily, 'otherwise I suspect my bank account would receive a battering.'

They all laughed, and Drew stood up. 'Holly hasn't checked out Chester yet, and I don't want to be back late. Simon wants to leave early tonight.'

Simon was one of the four men Drew employed on the farm, and Holly knew now that whenever one of them wasn't available it meant additional work for Drew himself. She felt guilty at taking up so much of his very precious time, but, when she said as much after they had said their goodbyes, he shook his head, telling her that she was being silly.

'I can't get over how much your mother's changed,' she marvelled.

'Yes, marriage to James suits her.'

'Drew...' She hesitated and then said quickly, 'I think your mother believes that you and I...well, that we're involved,' she said awkwardly.

'Involved?' He stopped walking and turned to stare at her, one eyebrow raised. 'Do you mean she thinks we're lovers?' he asked her drily.

'Well, yes.'

'And you want me to correct that misapprehension, do you, Holly? Hasn't it occurred to you that that's exactly what we don't want? You were the one who suggested we pretended to be in love,' he reminded her.

She said nothing. How could she? How could she explain to Drew how much she hated deceiving his mother? And how awful she had felt when she had asked her not to hurt him? She hadn't realised when they first embarked on this deception just what was going to be involved, she realised drily.

As an ex-bank manager, James had had several excellent suggestions to put to Holly as to how to conduct her search for premises, and had even offered to make covert enquiries among his business acquaintances, many of whom were connected with local business and property in one way or another.

Visits to a couple of local estate agents had soon ascertained that rentals in the better parts of the city were very high indeed, and Holly's face reflected her dismay when she and Drew left the third agent they had visited.

'To make enough profit just to pay the rent and rates, I'd have to make an outstanding success of the shop from the word go,' she told Drew glumly, 'and that just can't be done. It takes time to build up a good reputation. People pass on recommendations from work they have done or seen. Of course, advertising helps, but to cover those sort of costs...'

'Don't get downhearted,' Drew advised her. 'We haven't exhausted all the possibilities yet.'

But Holly wasn't listening to him. 'And then there's setting up the showroom as a display case for our work. In London Jan has a cabinet-maker who she used to fit out the shop with display cupboards for the fabrics, which I dragged and stencilled,' she explained to him. 'They look really effective and it shows people what can be achieved, and how high our standards are. It's fitted out as a sort of drawing-room-cum-study, and I know it cost the earth for the units.'

'Well, we could get round that problem easily enough. I'd be happy to build the units you need, Holly. That's if...'

'Oh, Drew! Would you?' Her face was alight with pleasure and relief, but then it fell again. 'But the time... and you so busy. I couldn't ask you to...'

'You wouldn't need to ask,' Drew pointed out wryly. 'I've already volunteered. Unless of course you're just being tactful, and my workmanship isn't of a high enough standard. It *is* only a hobby, after all.'

'Not *good* enough? Drew, those units in your kitchen are among the best I've ever seen!'

'Well, then, we've solved one problem, and we'll soon solve the others.'

We. How good that sounded, compared with Howard's lack of interest in her career.

A thought struck her. 'Does ... Does Rosamund work?' she asked diffidently. She was beginning to loathe the sound of the other woman's name, and not solely because of Howard. She hated mentioning her, because she hated hurting Drew, hated reminding him of what had happened.

'Hardly,' Drew replied drily. 'She doesn't really have time, what with the visits to the villa in Spain and the trips on the yacht. Besides ...'

Holly bit her lip. Poor Drew, and yet he sounded more contemptuous than distressed.

'Come on,' Drew announced abruptly, taking hold of her arm.

'Where are we going?'

'I thought we'd have afternoon tea at the Grosvenor. Take the weight off our feet for a few minutes. All this walking around is exhausting.'

Holly laughed at him.

'How can you say that?' she accused. 'And you a farmer.'

'Ah, but there's a difference between walking through fields and pounding hard pavements.'

The Grosvenor was pleasantly busy, most of the tables occupied by groups of smartly dressed women, expensive glossy carrier bags beside them denoting the nature of their shopping, although, as the waiter showed them to a table for two, Holly noticed that there were several other couples there, including one very young pair who, to judge from the way they were both studying the small diamond ring on the girl's slender finger, were just celebrating their engagement.

After consulting Holly as to her preferences, Drew gave their order. The service was excellent, Holly noted, as she sipped the fragrant and piping hot tea she had just poured. Drew had also ordered sandwiches, and, although she hadn't initially felt hungry, the sight of them tempted her to taste one.

When Drew urged her to have another, she protested half-heartedly that she was already guilty of being greedy, and that if she ate any more she would be putting on weight.

She was just hesitating between the salmon and the chicken when Rosamund's mother suddenly appeared beside them.

'Drew! I thought it was you. And . . . Polly, isn't it? My dear!' she exclaimed with false concern. 'How very brave you are. Sandwiches . . .' She gave a tiny shudder. 'I'm afraid I simply daren't. I have to watch my figure.' As she spoke, she smoothed one well-manicured hand over the slender line of her skirt. 'And of course it's so much worse when one's small, isn't it? One daren't allow oneself to get above an eight at the most. I suppose you must be a size twelve at least, Polly.'

Holly put down the sandwich and said quietly, 'A ten, actually,' but it was too late. Rosamund's mother had already made her feel uncomfortably conscious of the soft roundness of her figure. She wasn't plump, and indeed her ribcage and waist were very narrow, but she certainly didn't have the bone-thin slenderness of Rosamund and her family.

'So what are you doing in Chester, then?'

Her hard blue eyes stared at Holly's bare engagement finger, and Holly had to suppress a daunting urge to conceal her hand. She left Drew to answer, only just controlling her surprise when he said calmly, 'We've been to have lunch with my mother.'

Mrs Jensen looked rather taken aback, but she recovered swiftly and asked sweetly, 'Oh, and how are dear Louise and James? I must get in touch with them. Ah, I think my friends are ready to leave. Goodbye, Andrew.' She gave Holly a dismissive smile and hurried away to join the group of women waiting by the exit.

Her appetite totally gone, Holly stared down at her plate, her sight blurred by mortified tears. She suspected that Mrs Jensen would far rather have Drew as a son-in-law than Howard, and with her on his side she didn't see how Drew could possibly fail to win Rosamund back. Which would, of course, surely mean that Howard would turn to her, which was exactly what she wanted. Or was it?

'I take it you're not going to eat that?' Drew asked extremely drily, recalling her thoughts and making her take a deep, steadying breath. The very last thing Drew would want would be her bursting into tears all over him because Rosamund's mother had hurt her feelings.

'I was full up, anyway,' she told him lightly, her voice only trembling the tiniest little bit.

'So, what now?' Drew asked when they were outside once more. 'More groundwork, or home?'

Home. How blissful it sounded; and oddly enough the farm *had* become home to her. Even the farm dogs had stopped barking at her, as though readily accepting her right to be there. Of course, that was probably just because they were well trained, she reflected wryly, answering Drew's question with a quiet,

'Home, I think. I'd really like to get a few things down on paper, so that I can report back properly to Jan.'

'Well, don't lose heart yet,' Drew advised her. 'We've still got Knutsford and Nantwich to see. I can't take any more time off until Thursday, but if you like we could go into Knutsford then and have a look round.'

'Well, if my car comes back tomorrow, I can go by myself,' Holly pointed out.

'Well, of course, if that's what you'd prefer to do.'

Was that really a cool note of stiffness in Drew's voice, as though she had in some way offended him? Holly pushed the thought aside. Of course, it couldn't be. He was probably only too relieved to be freed from the necessity of accompanying her.

CHAPTER SIX

'I'VE brought your car back, miss. Everything's fine now...'

'Oh, thank you. I'm sorry you had to send for the spare. I suppose really I should have asked Drew to take it to a local dealer, but I just never gave it a thought.'

'Send for a spare? But...'

'Thanks, Jack. I take it everything's in order?'

Holly hadn't heard Drew arrive in the yard, and whatever the garage mechanic had been about to say was lost as he chatted to Drew and handed her car keys over to Holly.

After he had gone, Holly remarked, 'That's odd. He doesn't seem to have left me a bill. Perhaps he'll send it in the post.'

'It's all been taken care of,' Drew told her briefly, and it took Holly several seconds to realise what he meant.

'Drew, you haven't paid it!' she exclaimed in distress. 'Oh, you mustn't do that. Please give me the bill.'

'If you insist,' he said quietly, obviously a little taken aback by her insistence.

Holly followed him into his office, where he handed the bill over to her.

'What's the panic, Holly?' he asked her. 'Does it offend you that I paid it?'

'No. No... nothing like that,' Holly assured him. If she was honest with herself, she had rather liked the sensation of being cosseted and taken care of; indeed, she could very easily get all too used to it. Drew's manners were of the old-fashioned variety, but he was no domineering chauvinist, and Holly could quite see that he would think it no more than his duty to pay for the repairs, simply because he had been responsible for taking the car to the garage.

'You've already done so much for me, Drew. Carry on like this and you'll be turning me into a helpless female parasite.'

'Not you,' he assured her, and his words warmed her heart.

She had half hoped he would insist on her waiting until Thursday to visit Knutsford so that he could go with her, but he had done no such thing, and so as soon as Drew had assured herself that her car had been properly repaired she set out for the pretty market town.

Parts of Knutsford owed a great deal to the Italian influence of a certain architect, and when Holly had parked her car and was wandering around the small town, familiarising herself with its layout, she smiled a little to see the Italianate buildings in their late autumnal Cheshire setting.

Of course, the town also had its traditional half-timbered coaching house, and the narrow thoroughfare that was the town's main shopping street was lined with a jumble of Tudor and Georgian buildings, interspersed here and there with something more modern.

The estate agent she visited first was pleasant but dismissive: a man in his late fifties, who plainly was not prepared to take her seriously, and Holly longed to have Drew at her side. Drew was the kind of man who would instantly command respect and attention from other members of his sex, she recognised, and yet he treated everyone with courtesy, not like Howard, who sometimes made her cringe with his high-handed and sometimes unpleasant attitude towards others.

As though by some magical process, her thoughts conjured him up, for, as she turned a corner, Holly almost ran into Howard himself.

Rosamund wasn't with him, and he frowned a little as he saw Holly.

She didn't miss the way he stepped off the narrow pavement as though he was almost frightened of coming into contact with her. Instead of hurting her, the gesture made her angry and contemptuous.

'What's wrong, Howard?' she demanded bitterly. 'Frightened that someone might see us together and report you to Rosamund?'

His skin mottled unpleasantly. 'Don't be so ridiculous, Holly,' he snapped at her, but Holly noticed that he was quick to edge them both completely round the corner into the quiet side street. 'What are you doing here anyway?' he demanded brusquely. 'I thought you'd have gone back to London by now.'

What he meant was that *he* wanted her to go back to London.

It was like having blinkers ripped from her eyes, Holly acknowledged sadly, suddenly seeing him without the rosy warmth of her love. The Howard she had loved had just been an illusion, she recognised painfully, a creature of myth and fantasy, and not a real human being at all. The reality appalled her. The man standing in front of her now wasn't even someone she could like, never mind love.

'Drew asked me to stay,' she told him absently, trying to come to terms with her own abrupt recognition of the truth.

She didn't love Howard any more. She looked at him, and marvelled to discover that she felt nothing . . . nothing at all.

As though something in her cool, straight glance discomposed him, Howard flushed uncomfortably. 'Be careful, Holly,' he jeered at her. 'You know what they say about love on the rebound. What are you doing here in Knutsford, anyway?'

'Nothing that's any of your business, Howard, and now if you'll excuse me . . .'

As she walked away without a backward glance, Holly felt the most glorious sense of relief and freedom. Her spirits soared. She wanted to burst out into song, to laugh and dance down the street. She looked up at the sky and realised it was the most marvellous shade of blue. The sun was warm and gentle, the trees beautiful in their autumn dress, in fact the whole world, and this corner of it in particular, was the most wonderful, marvellous place there was.

She was smiling when she walked into the second estate agent's. He was a little more helpful than the first, and when she left the small market town a couple of hours later she felt a good deal more hopeful than she had done when she and Drew left Chester.

She drove home in high spirits, bursting to tell Drew about her day. Only, Drew wasn't there.

Peter, the taciturn cowman, who was the oldest of Drew's four employees and who lived in one of the pair of tied cottages owned by the farm, told her dourly that Drew had gone to a meeting.

'Said to tell you not to wait dinner,' he informed her. 'Said he wouldn't be back until late.'

Feeling deflated, Holly headed for the house. It was surprising how empty it felt without Drew. She wandered round the kitchen, trying to concentrate on the units. Her paintbrushes and other equipment had arrived that morning, and she ought by rights to use what was left of the day to start work on preparing a stencil. Something pretty, but not too pretty. Something appropriate for the room and the farm.

Out of the corner of her eye she saw the large chestnut tree beyond the window, its turning leaves ruffled by a gusting wind that seemed to have sprung up out of nowhere.

Some of the leaves whirled upwards in a scatter of golden brown. Chestnut leaves . . . chestnut candles in the spring, rich spears of pink and white flowers. Yes, that could be her theme, the white of the candle flowers, the green of the spring leaves and young boughs, the golden yellow of the searing autumn leaves.

Her fingers almost itched to start work, and she hurried upstairs to her room to collect her equipment. She had no easel, but the kitchen table would do for a drawing-board.

Within half an hour, Holly was totally absorbed in what she was doing, swiftly sketching outlines for the components which would eventually make up her stencil.

Not wholly satisfied with her drawings, she got up impatiently and walked to the kitchen window. What she needed was a handful of leaves; hers didn't look right at all, she decided despondently.

It was still light outside, and the chestnut tree was only a matter of two or three fields away at most.

Deciding against wasting time by changing into jeans and wellingtons, she went outside as she was. For her trip to Knutsford, she had worn her pleated skirt and toning sweater, and she was glad of their warmth when she realised how chilly the wind was. Luckily it was dry underfoot, and the gate to the first field yielded easily as she swung it open and then took care to close it behind her, even though she knew that Drew had no stock in it.

The small milk herd he kept had now been brought in for the winter, and she presumed that he had done likewise with the beef stock.

Beyond the immediate environs of the farmhouse and its well-established garden was a long line of modern cattle sheds which she knew Drew had had built in the last few years. There was a good deal more to farming, she was beginning to realise, than simply owning land and animals.

The chestnut tree was further away than she had thought, and her calves were aching a little by the time she had crossed the second field.

The wind, blowing unchecked from the Welsh hills, buffeted her, tangling her hair and blinding her with it, but at last she reached her destination and started to gather up some of the fallen leaves.

Engrossed in her task, it was several seconds before she realised that she and the tree weren't the sole occupants of the field. Standing less than ten yards away, watching her, was Drew's prize bull.

Scrambling unsteadily to her feet, she stared at it in horror. For a second neither of them moved, and then it made a brief charge toward her.

Holly screamed and dropped the leaves, running as fast as she could for the gate and safety, acting on instinct alone and nothing else. Why, oh, why hadn't she checked the field before she opened the gate? Behind her she could hear the thunder of the bull's hoofs as it pursued her.

Panic made her heart pound, adrenalin pumping frantically through her veins, so that she forgot everything other than her need to escape.

The gate was ahead of her. Open. *Open?*

'Holly!'

She heard Drew call her name and she screamed out thankfully to him through her tortured lungs. Her scream took her last reserve of energy, and as he came running toward her she flung herself thankfully into his arms, only somehow her foot slipped and she felt herself falling, her unprotected body hitting the hard earth with a blow that drove every bit of oxygen from her lungs.

The bull's hoofbeats shook the earth. Frantically she tried to get up, dimly aware of Drew's soothing voice and helping hands, and then mercifully everything blacked out.

When she came round she was lying safely on the other side of the gate, on Drew's Barbour. As she looked anxiously at the gate, Drew squatted down beside her.

'Holly, does anything hurt?'

'No,' she told him quaveringly, testing her limbs uncertainly, but when she struggled to sit up he pressed her back gently.

'You took quite a tumble,' he told her quietly. 'Just lie there for a minute until you come round properly. What happened?'

'I wanted some leaves ... I was doing my stencil. I thought the field was empty.' Her bottom lip trembled and her eyes filled with tears of shock and relief. 'I thought the bull was locked up.'

'The bull?' Drew turned his head, and Holly shuddered as she saw the animal on the other side of the gate, pawing at the ground and watching her balefully.

'Oh, Septimus. Yes ... Yes, I see.'

Had she not been feeling quite so dreadful, she would have seen the distinct twinkle in Drew's eye, but she had closed her eyes to ward off the peculiar feeling of light-headedness engulfing her.

Beyond the gate, the bullock, that Drew's cowman's wife had raised by hand after he'd lost his mother, bellowed mournfully, feeling unfairly deprived of his human companion and potential playmate, and Drew turned his attention back to the woebegone figure at his feet.

'Don't get up,' he told Holly comfortingly. 'I'll carry you back to the house. You've had a nasty shock. Oh, and don't worry about your skirt, it should clean up all right.'

'My skirt? Oh, yes, the mud when I fell.'

'Not mud, exactly,' Drew announced carefully.

Holly's eyes flew open. She touched the sticky mess adhering to the skirt tentatively, and winced as the smell told its own story.

'Oh, Drew! And I'm lying on your jacket!'

'Not to worry. Besides,' he added, 'it's only the front of you that—er—took the brunt of things.'

Ignoring Holly's despairing wails, he picked her up and carried her back to the house. No one else seemed to have witnessed what had happened, and Holly shuddered to think what the outcome would have been if Drew had not appeared.

She said as much, and, when he remained silent, added curiously, 'But what are you doing back? Peter said you wouldn't be until later.'

'The meeting of the church council I was due to attend has been cancelled. The vicar's been called to see the bishop on some urgent matter, and couldn't get a message through to us in time to stop us from turning up.'

'How long have you been on the council?' Holly asked him.

'Just over a year. The popular consensus of opinion was that it needed an infusion of young . . . well, relatively young blood. I was asked if I'd like to take on the job. We don't have any world-shaking decisions to make, but I find it very interesting.

'I think we'd better strip off your skirt and sweater in the kitchen, and then upstairs for a warm, reviving bath. Are you sure you don't want me to call out the doctor to check you over? That was quite a nasty tumble you took.'

'No, nothing's damaged. Bruised, maybe,' Holly admitted ruefully, 'but not damaged.'

To prove it, she tested her reflexes gingerly as he put her down, and then protested as he kneeled to unfasten the waistband of her skirt. 'Drew, I can do that.'

'I know, but it will be much quicker if I do it. You're still in shock, Holly,' he told her gently, 'and I think getting you out of these things is rather more important than maidenly modesty, don't you?'

'Umm... They do smell rather strong, don't they?' Holly agreed, hastily stepping out of her skirt as it dropped to the floor, and adding banteringly to cover her sudden self-consciousness, 'I'm surprised you haven't put me under the sluice in the yard as you do the dogs.'

Drew laughed. 'Ah, but they do it deliberately, *your* mishap was an accident. At least...'

He paused in his deft removal of her sweater to laugh down at her, and as she smiled back into his eyes Holly had the oddest sensation—just as though her heart had physically turned over in her chest and stopped beating.

In fact, so sure was she that it *had* stopped beating that she almost stopped breathing, only realising what she was doing from the sudden tightness of her chest.

'Holly, are you sure you're all right?' His smile changed to a frown.

'I'm fine,' she assured him huskily, summoning a smile as she added, 'At least, I will be once I've had that bath.'

'Mmm. I think I'd better carry you upstairs. We don't want to take any risk of your fainting again.'

'Drew, no! I can manage,' she protested, but he was deaf to her objections, picking her up easily, and

holding her in his arms as though he were completely
oblivious to the slim length of her bare legs and the
soft roundness of her body clothed only in the de-
mureness of her white lace bra and matching briefs.

'How did you get on in Knutsford?' Drew asked
her conversationally as they reached the top of the
stairs. For all the world as though they were sitting
having dinner, Holly thought crossly.

'Fine,' she told him curtly.

'Mmm. I believe Howard was there this afternoon.
You didn't happen to run into him, did you?'

Holly tensed in his arms. 'Yes, as a matter of fact
I did. How did you know he was there?'

'Oh, Rosamund told me,' he informed her carelessly, using his shoulder to push open the door not
to the bathroom she used but to the one adjacent to
his own room.

'Rosamund?'

'Yes. I saw her this afternoon when she dropped
her father off. He's on the council, too.'

'You saw her, and talked to her?'

The most appalling jealousy burned through her
like bush fire through overdry undergrowth. She had
never experienced anything like it in her life. It seared
and crackled, destroyed and wounded, and she shuddered under its bitter impact. She was *jealous* of
Rosamund, but not because of Howard. Oh, no...not
because of Howard. She was jealous of Rosamund
because...

'Hey...are you all right?'

The concerned question roused her from the turmoil
of her thoughts.

'Yes. Rosamund and Howard...'

'Oh, they're still engaged.'

She couldn't halt the fierce leap of relief inside her, and remorsefully she stretched out and curled her fingers round Drew's arm. For all that he strove to hide it behind his smile and careless words, he must be feeling dreadful. As dreadful as she was feeling herself, she acknowledged painfully.

And then she knew that she owed it to him to tell him the truth, and what was more to tell him what she was becoming more and more convinced was an impossible task. She herself no longer loved Howard, but she doubted that anything would make him give up Rosamund, nor her him. She owed it to Drew to tell him the truth.

'Drew,' she said hesitantly, 'I don't think our plan is going to work. I think we should accept that Howard and Rosamund are engaged and that they will get married. Anyway, I know now that I don't...'

'Give up?' Drew interrupted her. 'No way! No, we've got to keep on trying. You're just feeling down at the moment, Holly. You'll see things differently tomorrow,' he promised her. 'In fact, I'm sure you'll see things differently once you've had a bath and a hot meal. I'll run the water for you, and I'll give you half an hour to soak in it, then I'll come back for you. Scrambled eggs OK for supper?'

'Drew...'

'It will be all right, Holly. I promise you. Just have faith...'

And with that he put her down on a chair and dropped a light kiss on her hair as he released her and turned his attention to filling the old-fashioned bath with piping hot water.

'Half an hour, remember,' he warned her once he had assured himself that she could come to no harm getting in and out of the bath. 'And, Holly——' he paused at the door '—any problems . . . any feeling of faintness or anything . . . no false modesty, please. Just call out. I'll leave the door open.'

It was comforting to be so cosseted; comforting and . . . And yet the sensations inside her when Drew held her had nothing to do with comfort. Excitement, apprehension, awareness, aching physical desire. She had experienced all those things, and a multitude more.

She loved Drew. She sat in the bath, staring into space while her mind and heart absorbed the truth of the words.

But only a short time ago she had been equally sure that she loved Howard.

Ah, but then she had had no idea what love really was. What she had mistaken for love had been nothing more than a despairing clinging to an old habit. A need to have someone in her life she could care for.

With Drew, it was different. With Drew, she felt . . . she felt all woman, she acknowledged tremulously. With Drew, she just had to look at his mouth and her body trembled. He just had to touch her and . . .

'Holly, time's almost up!'

Frantically she scrambled out of the bath, drying herself hurriedly on a thick, fleecy towel.

Drew hadn't brought her any fresh clothes, and so, securing the towel around her body like a sarong, she padded to the top of the stairs just as Drew himself reached them.

'You didn't bring me any clothes,' she told him huskily, blushing a little beneath the open inspection he gave her pink shoulders and arms.

'No, I didn't, did I?' he agreed.

She had pinned her hair up on top of her head, and he touched an escaping wisp of black silk thoughtfully.

'You look like a deliciously wanton cherub, all innocent eyes and flushed skin,' he told her softly.

'Drew,' she protested breathlessly.

He looked at her and then said huskily, 'What is it you're asking me for, Holly? This?'

She murmured a denial, but it was too late, his arms were already around her, his mouth caressing the soft contours of hers.

How could she have ever thought she wasn't capable of feeling intense desire? she wondered hazily, as Drew bit gently at her mouth and then less gently as he felt her body's instinctive arch against his own.

His hands dug painfully into the soft, warm flesh of her upper arms but Holly barely noticed it. The aches and pains of her fall were forgotten, replaced by a deeper, more urgent ache.

She felt the hot coil of anxious pleasure begin to possess her body, and she moved instinctively against Drew. His hands moved to her shoulders and shaped her body, and she burned to feel their touch against her skin instead of merely through the blunting texture of the towel.

What had happened to her hesitancy, her reticence, her belief that physical pleasure was a kind of fulfilment that just wasn't for her?

A reckless, frantic urgency took hold of her, and as though he sensed and shared it Drew dragged her against his body, holding her there while his tongue circled the moist softness of her lips, tormenting her, and then eased between them, softly at first and then far more erotically as he recognised her responsiveness.

'Holly, I can't make love to you here on the stairs. Let me take you to my room.'

Make love to her... Her whole body shuddered with insane delight at the thought. She actually started to melt compliantly against him, and then abruptly reality intruded. Drew didn't want her; she was just a substitute for Rosamund, and she, fool that she was, had been idiotic to fall in love with him... That was the *last* complication either of them needed.

To her own consternation as much as Drew's, she burst into inexplicable tears, causing him to release her gently.

'I'm sorry,' she gulped. 'I think it's just the shock.'

'Of me having the temerity to want to make love to you?' Drew asked her drily.

Not daring to look up at him, and so missing the pain his light words concealed, Holly shook her head. 'No. Not that. It's the after-effect of being chased by your bull.'

And in fact she did feel decidedly shaky, her legs suddenly boneless and weak, and she would have subsided on to the floor where they stood, if Drew hadn't taken her in a steadying hold.

'Oh, Drew, I was so frightened,' she told him truthfully, not enlightening him that her fear sprang more from her discovery that she loved him than from her flight from the field. Now that she was once more in possession of her senses, she was desperately anxious to distract him from questioning her intensely passionate response to his kiss.

Everyone knew that men, those weak creatures, could be physically aroused by women they did not love, but women... well, they were different; and if she didn't occupy his thoughts with something else, Drew might well wonder why on earth she had responded to him so wantonly when she was supposed to be in love with Howard.

'I didn't realise your bull was in that field.'

'I've got a confession to make,' Drew told her. 'He wasn't.'

'He wasn't? But he chased me.'

Drew shook his head. 'No. *Septimus* chased you,' he corrected her. 'Come on, let's go downstairs and have our supper, and I'll explain.'

Bewilderedly, Holly let him guide her downstairs.

'I thought we'd eat cosily in the sitting-room tonight,' Drew announced. 'You go through—I'll bring it in. It's all ready.'

He had lit the fire in the small sitting-room off the kitchen, and the flames glowed warmly in the grate. Outside, the wind howled eerily, making the bare branches of the climbing roses tap and scratch at the windows.

Drew's scrambled eggs were delicious, but Holly had scant appetite for them. The day had brought too many shocks, and now she felt drained and tired.

'Tell me about Septimus,' she demanded, when she had eaten as much as she could.

Drew put down his knife and fork and gave her a wry look.

'Septimus is a bullock, not a bull...'

'Not a bull? But he must be! He had . . .' She broke off and flushed vividly, much to Drew's obvious amusement.

'Maybe, but he's still a bullock. He was hand-reared by Peter's wife after he lost his mother. The kids made quite a pet of him and he used to follow them around. He should have been sent off to market months ago, but somehow or other I hadn't the heart. He *wasn't* chasing you, Holly. He just thought you were a new playmate. He's lonely.'

'Oh!' Crimson with mortification, Holly stared miserably at him. 'You must think me an absolute fool,' she said quietly at last.

Instantly Drew reassured her, taking one of her hands in his and curling his fingers round her wrist. The sensation of his thumb against her pulse, absently stroking that vulnerable area, made it pound erratically.

'Not at all. I promise you I should have been equally terrified faced with crossing one of London's main roads without the benefit of traffic lights. There's nothing to be embarrassed about. I'm only sorry that you had such a bad fright. I should have warned you about Septimus's predilection for human companionship.'

'Oh, Drew, thank goodness no one else saw me! Your men . . .'

'They'd all gone . . . but they aren't insensitive, Holly. They would have understood.'

'Poor Septimus,' Holly said shakily with a light laugh. 'I suppose I gave him quite a shock, running away from him screeching like that.'

'Well, you can make amends some time if you feel up to it. I'll make a formal introduction.'

'Oh, Drew,' she said impulsively, reaching out with her free arm to touch his hand. 'You're so *nice*. Rosamund must be a complete fool.'

'For loving Howard?' Drew asked her, looking intently at her.

Immediately she crimsoned again, realising how idiotic her comment had been.

'Howard is Howard,' she said bravely. 'And you are *you*. You're two very different men. I—I... I might love Howard, but that doesn't mean that I can't see how... how...'

'How perfect I'd be for Rosamund,' Drew supplemented for her, his voice unusually harsh and bitter.

'I'm sorry,' she apologised. 'I shouldn't have said anything.'

'Why not? It's good to know the truth. Tell me something, Holly,' he said with sudden violence. 'If there was no Howard, then do you think I might be considered the perfect man instead of only second best?'

'Oh, Drew... you're not second best,' Holly protested, hating seeing him in such pain.

He gave her a long, brooding look, and then said harshly, 'I think I'd better go out and check on the stock... before I do something we'll both regret.'

Something like making love to her out of the frustration of his desire for Rosamund? Holly wondered hectically when he had gone.

Only she knew how shamingly tempted she had been to throw caution to the winds and offer herself to him, even knowing that the solace she could offer was purely temporary.

To have known his lovemaking only once...to have been close to him, part of him... But why torment herself? Wasn't it far wiser to keep Drew's friendship and her own self-respect, and to keep her love for him her own secret?

CHAPTER SEVEN

THE REST of the week passed without incident. Holly prepared her stencil and started work on the kitchen units, mixing her paint carefully until she was sure she had got exactly the right shade of yellow.

Then she made up a single door-panel from a spare piece of wood Drew had found her, so that she could show him what the finished effect would be.

His genuine and warmly given praise made her achingly conscious all over again of what a wonderful man he was. Warm, generous, compassionate, and yet at the same time very much a man. She shivered, remembering how she had felt when he kissed her, wondering how on earth she had managed to delude herself into believing she loved Howard for so long.

One morning he woke her early, just after six, and announced that they were going mushrooming. Holly complained bitterly as he flung back her duvet and opened the bedroom window so that the cold dawn breeze blew into the room, but Drew had also brought her a mug of fragrant coffee, and the thought of spending the mystical, special fresh morning hours with him was a far more tempting prospect than staying in bed.

He had warned her to dress warmly and wear wellingtons, explaining when she joined him downstairs that there would be a heavy dew on the fields. There was more than that; there was also a thick, shimmering mist that added to the eeriness of the landscape. As though he shared her awareness of the mystic quality of the morning, Drew put his hands on her shoulders and turned her round so that she was looking not at the Welsh hills, but at the sharp escarpment of Alderley Edge.

'Watch,' he told her. 'Once the mist starts to disperse you'll be able to see it properly. Have you ever been there?'

'Once,' she told him, shivering at the memory. 'With my parents. It was eerie. All those trees, and yet you never heard a bird sing or saw an animal move.'

'There's a legend that Merlin lives in a cave beneath the rock and that he's just waiting for the right time to reappear.'

'And covens of witches dance there on Hallowe'en. I know,' Holly added.

Her eyes were huge and slightly shadowed, and Drew cupped her face lightly in his hands.

'You look scared to death,' he told her softly. 'I'm sorry, I didn't mean to frighten you.'

'You didn't,' Holly managed a small, husky laugh. 'It's just that when I think of how old this land is ... how many people have been here before us ...'

'Yes, it is an awesome thought,' Drew agreed, immediately picking up on her thoughts. 'It comes to me when I'm in church and I see the tombs of the Norman knights who fought against the Welsh, and I remember that this land has seen much bloodshed and conflict. Sober thoughts for a fine autumn morning, and besides, we came out here to pick mushrooms, not to brood on the past.'

He looked down at her with a smile, and then his eyes darkened and Holly thought he was going to kiss her.

She wanted him to; she knew that. She wanted to be held in his arms, out here, wrapped in the mist that was dampening her hair as it rose. She wanted to be free to give in to her instincts and emotions, to show him with all the elemental awareness within her how passionately she loved him, but far away a dog barked sharply and Drew tensed and released her, lifting his head.

Holly could have cried out loud in vexation and disappointment, but instead she picked up the basket Drew had been carrying and said huskily, 'Right, then, where are these mushrooms?'

On the way back Drew introduced her to Septimus, who, despite his heavy, powerful frame, proved to be as docile and affectionate as Drew had said. Scratching his woolly forehead, Holly apologised to him for being afraid.

As they headed back to the farm, for no apparent reason at all Drew put his arm around her and hugged her tightly to his side. Taken off guard, Holly stared at him and wondered again how on earth Rosamund could prefer Howard. It didn't help knowing that until very recently *she* had almost been guilty of the same idiocy, but at least she had the excuse of not having known any better. Just this very short space of time with Drew had immediately revealed the truth to her.

Funny how, after all her emotional agonisings over her relationship with Howard, and her dogged determination to make the best of it with all its flaws, she had known the moment she realised she loved Drew how very different this love was from the feelings she had had for Howard. How she had known that her love for Drew would be a part of her life for ever, even though he himself might not be.

The wonder of it was that she had never realised the truth before, but then, as a teenager, she had seen him as Rosamund's boyfriend, and then later her visits home had not been for long enough for her to do more than catch up with her old schoolfriends. And although she had seen Drew and spoken to him, she had never spent much time alone with him.

They had the mushrooms for lunch in an omelette that Drew cooked, claiming that it was his speciality. In return Holly insisted that she was going to cook their evening meal. Not steak; making the acquaintance of Septimus had made her feel slightly reluctant to eat meat. Instead Drew drove her to the market at Chelford, where he himself had some business to conduct, and she amused herself exploring the various stalls, while Drew went off with another farmer he knew.

Two hours later, her arms laden with her purchases, Holly made her way back to the Range Rover. She had bought fresh salmon and tiny, sweet strawberries; from the eggs from Drew's hens she could make hollandaise sauce and meringue for the strawberries.

A stall selling home-made cheese and pâtés had tempted her, and she had ended up having a long discussion with the woman running it, a farmer's wife whose interest in the old-fashioned methods of cheese-making and farm husbandry had led her to setting up her own small business selling her produce.

Once, years ago, every small market town would have been like this, Holly recognised, and on market day the stalls would have been crammed with home-made local produce. She bought some matured local cheese, and the stallholder recommended a shop to her where she would find excellent local bakery bread.

Drew had reached the Land Rover ahead of her, and his eyebrows rose when he saw how laden she was.

'Bought up the entire market, have you?' he asked her humorously as he relieved her of some of her shopping.

'Not quite, but everything looked so tempting. What about you? Did your business go well?'

'I think so. The first lot of my bull's offspring are reaching the end of their first summer, and I wanted to know how well they're doing. He's a cross-bred bull, not generally favoured in this part of the world, and I took something of a chance in buying him, but so far the results are good.'

'Breeding animals sounds a complicated and risky business,' Holly commented as he helped her into the Land Rover.

'Oh, it is, especially in today's competitive markets. I hope you've got something for us to eat in these parcels, otherwise it's going to have to be steak.'

He was obviously amused by her refusal to eat the meat, and yet his amusement was kind, as though he understood how she felt.

When she said as much, he laughed in agreement. 'I'll never forget the time my mother bought some geese for fattening. Not one of us could touch our Christmas lunch that year.'

'Well, I've bought salmon for supper,' Holly told her.

She hadn't seen either Rosamund or Howard since her visit to Knutsford, and, oddly, the other couple and the purpose of Holly staying with Drew had totally disappeared from their conversation.

After dinner, when Drew asked if she would like to go out, either in to Chester, or alternatively to the local pub, Holly shook her head and stretched lazily in her chair. She was quite content where she was, and Drew must be feeling the same way too, because he made no mention of the fact that several days had gone by without their making any attempt to foster jealousy in Rosamund and Howard.

Only one thing spoiled what had otherwise been a perfect day, Holly reflected sleepily as they went upstairs, and that was that she and Drew were going to separate rooms. She shivered a little, acknowledging how easily she had slipped into the delusion of believing her life here was infinite, that she was a permanent part of Drew's life, when in reality...

She hesitated on the stairs, torn by conflicting feelings. Common sense told her that the wisest thing she could do now would be to tell Drew that she had fallen out of love with Howard and say that she need no longer continue the deception. She could then move out of the farm, and perhaps find an inexpensive hotel near Chester which she could use as a base while she looked for a venue for Jan's new shop.

But when did common sense ever mean anything to a woman in love?

Seeing her pause and sway slightly on the stairs, Drew offered teasingly, 'Want me to carry you to bed, sleepyhead?'

Did she? Her heart did a whole range of somersaults, worthy of an East European gymnastics champion. For a moment she was desperately tempted. Drew liked her, he liked kissing her; he was a very male man, missing the woman he loved. His body could be aroused by the feminine softness of her own, Holly already knew, and once she was in his arms, once he was making love to her, might it not be possible that she could make him forget Rosamund?

A cold wash of horror swept her as she realised what she was contemplating. How contemptible she would be if she allowed him to do that ... if she encouraged him to do it, knowing that he loved someone else, and knowing that he would doubtless feel contrite and embarrassed once the lovemaking was over. What kind of person was she to even think of encouraging something like that to happen?

The kind who had suddenly discovered that she was desperately in love with a man she knew she was soon to lose. There was a kind of despairing poignancy about every moment they spent together now, an endless yearning that possessed her to treasure every single second; an aching need to reach out and tell him how she felt, contradicted by the voice of reason warning her that it was neither fair nor wise of her to inflict her own feelings on Drew, especially not when he must be missing Rosamund more desperately with every day that passed.

Not that he betrayed it; not that he ever made Holly feel that he didn't enjoy every single moment of their time together; but that just went to show how kind and considerate he was.

'Pick me up? Carry me to bed?' she teased in as cheerful a rallying tone as she could manage. 'After all the food I've eaten recently? Somehow I don't think that would be a good idea. I'm not like Rosamund,' she added, and her voice betrayed her, hardening fractionally with jealousy.

'A perfect size eight?' Drew asked derisively, immediately realising what she meant. 'She's too thin. Don't try to change yourself, Holly. You're perfect as you are.'

Dizzy with pleasure, she looked up at him, and her breath locked in her throat. He was going to kiss her, she knew he was. They had reached the top of the stairs, and, as though she had stepped outside herself and was watching Drew and herself like two figures moving in slow motion, she saw Drew reach for her, and knew her own body melted compliantly toward him, aching for the hard warmth of him against it. The cuff of his woollen shirt brushed her face as he lifted his hand to push her hair away and cup her jaw. His eyes burned dark like those of an eagle, and her breath was released on a jerky, tense gasp.

'Holly.'

He said her name softly, like a benediction, and her eyes closed as she felt the soft movement of his thumb against her mouth, rubbing tormentingly at her lips.

She swayed toward him and felt his free arm go round her, drawing her into the heat of his body.

'Holly.'

His hand turned her face, his head came down, his thumb parting her lips as he slid his own between their moist softness, tasting, teasing, filling her senses with the taste, the feel, the scent of him.

His mouth tasted faintly of the brandy they had had with their coffee, and she touched his lips with her tongue, hazily pursuing the elusive flavour.

She heard him moan, a fierce, hoarse sound of male desire that made him seem almost alien, not the Drew she knew at all. Beneath her hand she could feel the furious beat of his heart, and his fingers where they gripped her waist were almost bruising the soft skin. He moved, taking her with him, leaning back against the wall and manoeuvring her between his thighs, groaning as his hand moved to her spine, pressing her against his aroused flesh.

Her heart thudding so frantically that she could hardly breathe, Holly leaned into him; this was fate's doing and not hers. She need feel no guilt, no remorse.

Drew's hand cupped her breast, pushing aside the silk covering of her blouse, and she whimpered softly, blind . . . drunk on love and desire.

'Holly! Holly, I've got to see you . . . touch you . . . taste you.'

She didn't hear the words, only the anguished sound of his voice and its need, a need that matched her own . . . that mirrored her own. She sighed with impatient acquiescence as he unfastened her blouse and pushed it from her shoulders. His hands trembled as he unsnapped her bra. The light at the top of the stairs was dim, throwing shadows over her soft flesh.

She felt Drew's chest lift and then fall sharply, recognising in the bemused awe of his gaze that he was paying her the highest compliment it was possible for a man to pay a woman's body.

'I knew you'd be beautiful,' he told her huskily, 'but not like this, so perfect that ...'

Instinctively Holly arched back, obeying the feminine force within her, just as instinctively cradling Drew's dark head in her hands as he placed tender lips against the curve of her body. His hair felt like silk beneath her fingers, the bones beneath it hard and male.

She trembled as she felt the warmth of his mouth against her skin. Gentle as a breath; tormentingly arousing.

And then, cruelly, her mind reminded her of the truth. Drew didn't love *her* ... he loved Rosamund. Instinctively she pulled away. She felt Drew resist and then let her go. His face was flushed with passion, his body tense and hard.

'Drew, we mustn't,' she told him huskily. 'It isn't right.'

For a moment she thought he intended to overrule her, to pick her up and simply carry her to his bed, but then, as though he had mastered the impulse, he stepped back from her and said quietly, 'You're right. It isn't. That's the trouble with propinquity, isn't it, Holly? It doesn't always work the way we want it to.'

As she watched him walk down the landing to his bedroom, Holly had to squash an appalling wish that he *had* overruled her, that he had ignored her and simply gone on making love to her. But what good would it have done?

It would have eased the unremitting ache inside her, Holly acknowledged frankly. It would have given her a taste of heaven, if only briefly. It would have allowed her to be one with him, to share pleasure with him, to give him the gift of her love, even if he didn't realise he was receiving it. But now it was too late.

She had to suppress an urge to run after him and tell him that she had changed her mind, but wisely she managed to stop herself.

The weather had changed. Outside the wind blustered, dashing yellowed leaves against the window. Holly had been awake for a long time. Today she and Drew were having lunch with his mother at Rookery Hall. She was glad that Jan had sent on one of her favourite dresses, a simple fine wool crêpe in red with a neatly fitted bodice and a short, straight skirt gathered from a slightly lowered waistband. It was at once both demure and teasingly provocative. It suited her curvy shape, and Holly knew she looked good in it. She had a black velvet three-quarter jacket she could wear over it.

As she lay there, desperately trying to fill her thoughts with everything bar her memories of last night, she heard footsteps outside the door. Drew must be up, even though he had told her that they did not need to get up early since one of his cowmen had agreed to stand in for him.

She pushed back the duvet and swung her feet to the floor just as he opened the door, startling her a little because she had thought he was on his way downstairs. She was even more startled when he came over to the bed and said firmly, 'I need your help.'

He was wearing a towelling robe, and his hair sprang damply from his scalp. She could smell the fresh, clean scent of his soap and shampoo, and as he caught hold of her hand and tugged her to her feet she saw the fine covering of dark hair shadowing his chest.

Her stomach lurched protestingly. What was the matter with her? she chided herself despairingly. She had seen Howard's chest often enough, and it had never, ever had this effect on her.

'Drew, what is it? What's wrong?' she asked him as she followed him out of the room and along the corridor in the direction of his own bedroom.

'Nothing's wrong,' he told her as he opened the door and gave her a gentle push inside. 'I just need to know what I should wear today.'

'What you should wear?' Holly stared at him.

'Yes. You know... my new clothes. I know you told me what goes with what, but I'm afraid I've forgotten, and I've probably got them all mixed up anyway.'

'You brought me in here to choose your clothes?'

'Yes, that's right,' Drew agreed cheerfully. 'I thought it would be easier than bringing the stuff to your room.'

'But, Drew, I'm not dressed.'

He looked at her then, and Holly wished she hadn't drawn his attention to her unclothed state as she saw the way his glance rested momentarily on the full thrust of her breasts beneath her cotton nightshirt.

'No, I should have thought of that,' he agreed. Before she could say a word, he whisked the duvet off his bed, and bundled her into a chair, tucking it round her.

'There, that should keep you warm enough.'

Warm? That wasn't what she had meant at all. The scent of his body clung to the duvet cover, tormenting her. It seemed too much of an effort to continue to protest, and, besides, what was the point?

'I've got everything in here,' Drew told her, his back to her as he opened the wardrobe doors.

He reached in and extracted one of the shirts they had bought, and then, before Holly could stop him, stripped off his robe and flung it on to the bed.

He was wearing a pair of boxer shorts, surely far briefer than those she had seen modelled on the pages of magazines. Or was it simply that Drew...? She swallowed hard and tried to control her tumultuous thoughts. Drew's body was powerfully developed by his life-style, and of course it was only logical that he, as an adult male of close on thirty, should have a much more powerfully built frame than the teenage models chosen by the magazines.

Even so, Holly found herself desperately looking everywhere but at his body. But the temptation was too much for her. Surreptitiously she watched as he reached out for the shirt and the shorts slipped a little lower on his hips.

He turned round unexpectedly, catching her staring, but seemed unaware of it, and of the reason for her suddenly strangled breath as he shrugged on the shirt and the corded muscles of his chest and belly hardened. The fine, dark hair covered not only his chest, but ran downwards in a dark line disappearing into his shorts.

Her mouth had gone dry, and Holly touched her lips with her tongue, wondering why she should find it so difficult to breathe.

'What do you think?' Drew asked her, and it took her several seconds to focus on his shirt and realise what he was asking.

'Well, it looks fine, Drew... but what are you planning to wear with it?'

'These trousers,' he told her, producing the plain pair they had bought. 'And the tweed blouson.'

With a struggle, Holly forced her mind to concentrate.

'Wasn't there a blue shirt?' she asked him, remembering that she had suggested buying one. 'It had tiny buttons, I think.'

'Ah. Here it is,' Drew told her, rifling through the wardrobe and producing it.

It was still in its plastic covering, and he struggled with it for a few seconds before bringing it over to her and asking, 'Can you help with this? I can't seem to get into it.'

'You do it like this,' Holly told him wryly, peeling back the self-sticking flap, and then realising, as she handed it back to him, how very close to her he was. Far too close for comfort, especially when he insisted on staying there while he removed his shirt, his body flexing sinuously with every movement.

This was pure torture, sitting here, watching him while she ached to reach out and touch him.

He seemed to have no embarrassment or self-consciousness at all about walking about in front of her in just his shorts, but then of course he was used to this sort of intimacy. He and Rosamund...

Jealousy rose up inside her, hot and bitter, and she was glad when his outfit was finally chosen and she was free to escape to her own room.

As she reached the door, Drew stopped her, reaching out and touching her arm. It was just a touch, no more than the brief laying of the warmth of his palm and fingers against her skin, but it made her shudder wildly and turn to him, her eyes dark with fear and reaction.

'Holly, what is it? What's wrong?'

He looked and sounded so concerned; another minute and she would be flinging herself into his arms, telling him all the things that could not and must not be said, telling him that she loved him and that Howard had faded from her mind so completely that she could barely conjure up his features, begging him to try to forget Rosamund and love her instead.

'It isn't because of last night, is it?' he asked her gently.

'No . . . no, it isn't that.'

'Ah, so there is something,' he pounced. 'What is it, then?'

This was unbearable, being so close to him, needing to be even closer, tormented by the far too vivid mental images of his near-nude body. She had to stop him questioning her, she had to escape before . . . before it was too late.

'I don't know. Nothing . . . I suppose I'm just not used to being around a half-dressed man,' she told him wildly.

He was silent, but she felt the odd, hard pressure of his fingers biting into her skin, as though what she had said had shocked him. As well it might. She shivered again and he released her, saying softly, 'Look at me, Holly.'

She didn't want to, but she found it impossible to resist the soft command. His eyes glowed warm gold, and she ached to reach out and touch her fingers to the hard planes of his face, to place her lips against the firm warmth of his, to...

'Does it disturb you?'

Half mesmerized, she jerked her head away, her mouth dry with panic.

'No... yes... Oh, Drew, the time,' she gabbled thankfully, as the grandfather clock chimed, splintering the intense tension surrounding them. 'I must get ready, otherwise we'll be late.'

He watched her dart into her bedroom with a wry look in his eyes.

He had always considered himself to be a patient man, but there were times... He flexed his muscles tiredly. The fault was his, but he hadn't been able to resist the impulse to tease her just a little, especially after last night.

Last night had left him raw and aching, and suddenly impatient with himself and with life. Sighing faintly, he made his way downstairs.

CHAPTER EIGHT

HOLLY dressed for lunch in the red dress that showed off her petite figure, and heightened the impact of her dark hair and pale skin.

She wore the pearl ear-rings which had been a twenty-first present from her parents, and the slim gold bangle which had been her coming-of-age gift from her brother, as though somehow these symbols of parental and fraternal love would give her courage and protect her.

Protect her? From Drew? No, from herself. She shivered again, conscious of how very close she had come to making a fool of herself. How embarrassed Drew would have been if she had broken down and confessed her change of heart. Thank goodness she had been able to stop herself in time.

The early morning mist had cleared to reveal a pale blue sky from which the sun shone brightly, but with very little warmth.

As they drove to Nantwich, the hollows untouched as yet by the sun rimed with frost, Holly decided she was glad she had brought with her the jacket to wear over her dress.

As she watched the scenery flash past she remembered how Drew had looked at her when she came downstairs: there had been an odd look in his eyes, something that had made her heart kick frantically in her chest, and her nerve-endings tighten.

'We'll be in Nantwich soon now,' Drew told her. 'You know, of course, that the "wich" part of the town's name derives from Roman times and the salt they extracted from the area.'

'Yes. Nantwich, Middlewich and Northwich were all Roman salt towns, weren't they?' Holly agreed.

It had been some years since she had visited the small town, and she was impressed by the influx of attractive shops that Drew's mother pointed out to her when they met the other couple at the designated spot.

After a brief walk round the town, Drew announced that it was time to drive to the manor house where they were having lunch.

As they walked back to the cars, Holly reflected that Nantwich could very probably be the right venue for the new shop. It had an ambience she had instantly liked, and the proximity of Rookery Hall, with its exclusive clientele, plus the influx of attractive small shops, added up to a very favourable impression.

If Drew's stepfather was right in saying that prices in the area were still very reasonable, she could well have found a home for the new outlet. And for herself? That was something else she would have to consider. A property that was two- or even three-storeyed would be ideal, and she could perhaps even combine her home with potential showrooms, for those clients who were genuinely interested in using their services.

She was so busy mulling over all the salient facts that she didn't realise they had reached the Range Rover until Drew said drily, 'Come back, Holly. We're here.'

She flashed him an apologetic smile, remembering how irritated Howard had always been by her enthusiasm for her work, but there was no anger in Drew's eyes, only an amused acceptance.

'I'm sorry. I hadn't realised how much Nantwich had changed. I was getting carried away with my mental plans.'

'You think it will be a good venue, then?'

'Yes. Especially if property prices are reasonable.' She chewed on her bottom lip. 'If I could, I'd like to buy the property myself... as my contribution to my partnership. I don't know if it could be done, though.'

'That's something you'll have to talk to James about. He's well up on the kind of business loans that are available.'

It wasn't far to Rookery Hall, and Holly, who had never visited the restaurant before, caught her breath in pleasure as they drove toward the house.

Set in its own grounds, and converted by the enthusiasm and hard work of its present owners into an exclusive small hotel and restaurant, it had the reputation of providing gracious and comfortable surroundings to the discerning diner.

They were made very welcome by the head waiter, and shown to a table with a marvellous view over the grounds. Menus were handed to them, and Holly's eyes widened a little as she studied hers.

The very attractive dining-room was virtually full, the other diners in the main being family groups: parents and grandparents with well-dressed, slightly subdued children, no doubt warned to be on their best behaviour, Holly reflected, smiling as she caught the eye of one little blonde cherub in a smocked velvet dress with white collar and cuffs.

A waiter appeared to take their order. Drew's mother leaned across the table to compliment Holly on her dress, and as she did so a foursome was shown to a table several feet away from their own.

Out of the corner of her eye, Holly caught a glimpse of Howard's familiar features and her heart sank, jealousy drowning out her pleasure in the day, as Rosamund detached herself from her parents and Howard, and came over to their table, smiling very prettily at Drew's mother and stepfather, and standing at their table in such a way as to have her back to Holly, and totally exclude her from the conversation.

Jealousy, like sharp knives, tore into her. She saw Rosamund reach out and touch Drew's arm, and she was appalled by the strength of her own desire to push the other girl away. Rosamund had no right to touch Drew, she was engaged to Howard . . . She ought to be with him, not over here, making eyes at Drew, speaking to him in that low, caressing voice that made Holly want to grind her teeth in anger.

She was talking about the countess's birthday party now, asking Drew if he was going, saying something about the possibility of her having to go without a partner, because Howard would be away on business with her father. She was actually all but inviting Drew to escort her, Holly realised fiercely.

Some women were like that, she knew, keeping their past lovers dancing on a string, reluctant to let them go, even though they had been supplanted. It was obvious to Holly that Rosamund was thoroughly enjoying flirting with Drew, and it wasn't for Howard's benefit, she acknowledged miserably, because he was deep in conversation with Rosamund's father, apparently oblivious to the behaviour of his fiancée. Why on earth didn't he look up, and come over and take Rosamund away? Why on earth didn't Drew send her away? Holly asked herself fiercely, totally forgetting the original purpose of her supposed involvement with Drew.

It was only the waiter arriving with their first course that reluctantly made her take her leave of them, but not until she had said coaxingly to Drew, 'Why don't we all have coffee together after you've finished your meal? Mummy was saying only the other day how long it is since she's seen you.'

Holly couldn't stand it. Without giving a thought to the consequences she placed her own hand on Drew's arm, only vaguely aware of its faint betraying tremble and the odd look Drew gave her, all her attention concentrated on Rosamund as she said huskily, 'Drew, darling, you promised me you'd show me the grounds after lunch.'

Rosamund glared at her and Holly held her breath, her pale skin flushing as she realised that everyone was looking at her, and that, moreover, what she had just said and done in no way fitted in with the plans that she and Drew had originally made.

Rosamund was jealous. She ought to be feeling pleased, to be congratulating Drew on his success, but all she could feel was an awful, burning ache, and a fierce desire to make Rosamund disappear, if possible for ever.

'I'm sorry, Rosamund. I did promise Holly a walk through the gardens. Perhaps another time.'

Defeated, Rosamund stalked off, but not before she had given Holly a furious look of hatred.

Bending her flushed face a little, Holly was thankful for Drew's mother's kind tactfulness when she said calmly, 'This soup is absolutely delicious. Do taste it, Drew, before it gets cold.'

Despite the calming effect of Drew's mother's presence, despite the businesslike conversation of James, his stepfather, as he discussed the pros and cons of Nantwich as a base for the business, Holly could not recover her earlier equilibrium.

All her pleasure in the day was destroyed by the fact that she knew that Rosamund was sitting not six yards away from them.

She was thankful that she had her back to the other group, but Drew did not, and she couldn't help wondering how many times Rosamund managed to catch his eyes, and how much he was wishing he could be with the other girl. Not that he betrayed those feelings. He was too kind, too polite for that, but he must have them, none the less. Rosamund was the woman he loved. He must be aching to be with her. He must be cursing Holly for butting in with that possessive comment.

Rosamund was obviously jealous and resentful of their relationship, but jealous enough to break her engagement with Howard? And that was what Drew would demand. He was not the man to play second fiddle to someone else, no matter how much he loved Rosamund.

These and other gloomy thoughts possessed her as Holly tried to pretend she was enjoying the meal. All around her people were talking and eating, but she felt as though she were isolated in a pool of misery from which there was no escape.

Drew addressed several comments to her, but she could only respond to them in monosyllables, so convinced was she that he must be absolutely furious with her.

The day which had started out so well was turning into a disaster, and she could hardly believe it when she looked out of the window and saw that the sun was shining, for her own thoughts were so grey and unhappy.

She barely touched her main course, her stomach knotted in sick nerves of distress. She saw Drew look at her, and put down her knife and fork, starting to tremble. She had always hated rows and arguments, and as a child the very thought of someone being angry with her had been enough to make her physically sick.

It was something she thought she had outgrown, but now her stomach was churning desperately and she longed to be anywhere but in this restaurant alone in her misery while all around her people laughed and chatted.

'Holly.'

The sound of Drew's quiet voice made her tense.

'Holly, you don't look well. Is something wrong?'

He sounded so kind and concerned, she longed to burst into tears. He must know what was wrong. How guilty and miserable she felt!

She looked up and realised that not just Drew, but his mother and stepfather were also watching her with concern. She was spoiling their lunch, turning what should have been a pleasant occasion into something very uncomfortable. Taking a deep breath, she forced a bright smile and assured him, 'No...not really. I think it's just that my eyes were much larger than my tummy.' Deliberately not allowing herself to give in to the hovering ache of self-pity, she said brightly to Drew's mother, 'I'm really impressed with Nantwich. I think it will make an ideal base for the business. I'm dying to get Jan up here to see it.'

'And I'm dying to get your help and advice with our guest suite,' Louise surprised her by saying. 'I've been threatening to do something with it ever since we moved into the house, and so far I haven't. Now I've had a letter from Lucy saying that she expects to be able to fly home for Christmas and that she's bringing a friend with her.'

'A friend?' Drew asked.

'A young man she's known for some time, apparently,' his mother responded quellingly when he grinned. 'Naturally I don't want her to feel ashamed of us and her home.'

'Come off it,' Drew teased his mother. 'That's just an excuse and you know it.'

His mother looked faintly pink.

'Well, it *does* need redecorating,' she said defensively. 'And I was wondering if Holly could do something very special and clever with the bathroom.' She made a wry face and said to Holly, 'The one good thing about it is that the sanitaryware is white, but the bathroom itself is very dull and so is the bedroom. I've got several ideas I want to talk over with you. In fact, I was going to suggest I come out to the farm one day next week.'

Holly jumped at the opportunity to banish Rosamund from her thoughts and make up for her earlier lapse. She was free to see her any day she cared to choose, she assured Drew's mother.

'And it will give you an opportunity to see what I've done to Drew's kitchen.'

'Hang on just a minute,' Drew protested, looking with mock severity at his mother. 'I can't have you taking Holly away from her work . . . and besides, I was thinking of asking her to do something about *my* bathrooms while she's here. I'm afraid you're just going to have to wait in line, Ma,' he told her with a grin.

Holly's mouth opened in a round 'O' of surprise.

'You didn't say anything to me about your bathrooms,' she protested.

'No. Well, I was waiting to choose my moment,' he told her with a smile. 'I thought I'd try and get my order in before you open the new shop and become too expensive for me.'

'I haven't finished the kitchen yet,' Holly reminded him. 'You might not want me to do your bathrooms when I have.'

To her astonishment he reached out and touched her face gently, cupping her jaw in the warmth of his palm.

'That's my Holly,' he said softly. 'Always the self-doubter.'

Beneath his hand her skin burned and a tiny pulse started to beat frantically. Her eyes dilated and darkened, her body trembling with an inner yearning she was powerless to control.

She was completely oblivious to the complacent look Drew's mother exchanged with her husband, and to the sudden tension in Drew's body as he felt her response. She only saw that his eyes darkened and glowed as he looked at her, and that a slow and very male smile warmed their topaz depths. The light caress of his palm against her sensitive skin made her body tingle, and she was completely oblivious to everything but him.

'Drew, if you and Holly have finished your lunch, why don't you show her the grounds?' his mother suggested lightly.

Both of them turned to look at her, as though surprised to find her there with them.

'But Drew hasn't had his coffee yet,' Holly blurted out, suddenly shy of being alone with him.

'I'm sure he won't mind,' his mother responded with a dry irony that was lost on both of them.

'Yes. Come on,' Drew said, standing up and drawing her with him. 'And while we're out there I'll do my best to persuade you to give your magic touch to my bathrooms, before Ma tempts you away. So be warned,' he said to his mother.

'Do you really want me to redecorate your bathrooms?' Holly asked, breathless, as he led her outside.

'Yes, but not as much as I want to kiss you,' Drew told her in an odd, thick voice that made her stare at him in confusion and surprise, thus giving him the opportunity to draw her into the shelter of a stand of tall conifers.

'Drew,' she protested uncertainly, but he was already touching her, already drawing her against the heat of his body, his hands stroking her, his mouth caressing hers gently, and then with a sudden, fierce urgency that sent thrills of arousal piercing through her as she clung to him, and responded to the demanding heat of his mouth with reckless intensity.

One part of her mind recognised how well he had tutored her in that her mouth clung pliably and longingly to his, obeying its every command, sensitive and responsive to his touch in a way that she had never been to Howard's.

It was only when she opened her eyes, dizzy with desire and delight, that she realised that they were within full sight of the dining-room. Flushing, she tried to point it out to him, but he was still kissing her, tiny, cherishing kisses that teased her throat and face, making her so weak that she had to cling to him to prevent herself from falling down.

'Drew, no,' she murmured as he tried to turn her face and slide her mouth under his. 'Everyone can see us.'

She just managed to get the words out as his lips feathered tormentingly against her own, and it wasn't relief but disappointment that roared through her when he stopped kissing her and raised his head.

'Sorry,' he apologised huskily. 'But it just seemed too good an opportunity to resist.'

Instantly she went cold with shock and the realisation that he had been kissing her quite deliberately, knowing that they would be seen... that he had wanted them to be seen.

There was no reason at all why she should feel this sense of betrayal, she told herself sternly. In Drew's eyes, he was simply reinforcing the impression that they had agreed that they would create, simply making the most of the moment to deliberately encourage Rosamund's jealousy.

And the other woman *had* been jealous. Holly had recognised that emotion in her immediately, probably because it so closely mirrored her own.

He hadn't kissed her because he desired her at all, and all that urgency and need she thought she had sensed within him had been either manufactured or the product of her own imagination. It wasn't Drew's fault she was feeling so hurt, so cheated. He hadn't meant to be unkind. He simply had no conception of how she felt about him, or how far she had strayed from the original path they had plotted out together.

No, he wasn't to blame for her present anguish. *She* was. She knew how she felt about him and she had known for some time. She swallowed hard and shivered. Instantly, Drew frowned.

'You're cold. That's my fault . . . I should have realised how chilly the wind is. Would you like me to go and get your jacket for you?'

Suddenly she ached to be alone, to be away from the disturbing effect of his presence. She nodded, numbly aware of the concerned look he was giving her. Was Rosamund having second thoughts, or was she simply angry because she considered Drew her exclusive property and resented him paying attention to anyone else? Would her anger be strong enough to make her break with Howard or . . .?

But she isn't good enough for him, Holly protested inwardly. She won't make him a good wife. She won't love him the way I would.

She tensed abruptly. What *was* she thinking? Was she really foolish enough to imagine, even in her most private thoughts, that she could be Drew's wife? What folly! What stupidity.

'If you walk down that path it will bring you out at a very pretty and sheltered fish pond. I'll meet you there, shall I?'

She nodded again, only half hearing Drew's words, so monstrous was her inner pain.

It struck her now as ironic to realise that the cause of her present misery was her imagined love for Howard. To look back at herself as the girl who had imagined herself in love with him was like looking down a long, distorting tunnel, and the person at the other end of it was so unfamiliar to her now that she could only marvel at her own naïveté and ignorance.

She hadn't had the remotest conception of what love really was, of what pain was. But she did now.

Drew was taking a long time. She walked back down the path and stopped abruptly as she saw Drew standing at the end of it with Rosamund and Howard. Rosamund was talking to him, smiling at him, while Howard hung back. What was she saying to him? What did it matter? Drew loved her, and so whatever she said or didn't say was probably immaterial to her own misery. Love wasn't born out of logic or reality, as she had good cause to know.

Drew turned his head and caught sight of her. She watched as he terminated the conversation and came toward her with his long countryman's stride.

Her heart pounded with pleasure. She ached to rush to meet him, to fling herself into his arms. Even his prosaic words of apology for keeping her waiting seemed special, cherishing, as though he really did care that she might have been cold; but he didn't tell her what Rosamund had been saying and, in the end, unable to stand it any longer, she asked huskily, 'What did Rosamund want?'

She couldn't look at him, so she pretended to be studying the view; a crisp, teasing breeze had sprung up out of nowhere, blowing her hair into her eyes. She lifted her hand to restrain it, but Drew was before her, his fingers warm against her cold skin.

'I'm sorry,' she apologised miserably. 'I shouldn't have asked. At least our plan seems to be working.'

It only needed Drew to agree enthusiastically to complete the misery, but instead he said casually, 'You should have joined us, reminded Neston of what he's missing.'

Holly gave a hollow laugh.

'He was watching you,' Drew told her curtly, surprising her both that he had noticed, and that for some reason he sounded angry. Surely he ought to have been pleased?

'Come on,' he said more gently, 'You're getting cold. Let's go inside.'

'Back to the town centre?' Drew's mother enquired when they rejoined them. 'Or have you had enough?'

'I'm taking her straight back home,' Drew replied for her, startling her a little with his firmness. 'It's my fault, but she's chilled to the bone. I'd forgotten that city living has softened her up, and she's not used to our cold winds.'

'Yes, you do look chilled,' his mother agreed, studying Holly closely.

'Oh, no, really,' Holly protested. 'I'm fine.' But no one seemed to be listening to her. Drew had put his arm round her as they left the dining-room, and now he tucked her against the warmth of his own body, holding her there.

It made her feel safe and secure, which was surely the most ridiculous piece of self-deception there ever was, but she felt too drained to resist the temptation of nestling close to him, letting the conversation drift over her as he and his mother discussed his sister's forthcoming Christmas visit.

'I don't know when you two are planning to get married,' she added casually. 'But if there's any chance of you arranging it for when she's over... She's staying for almost two months.'

Married! Holly felt her heart leap like a spawning salmon, her pulses racing frantically as she struggled to make some response, but once again Drew answered for her, his own voice slightly strained as he told her, 'It all depends when Holly's parents can come home.'

'Of course. But a winter wedding is so romantic, I think, and with your colouring, Holly...'

She sighed a little, and Holly felt an urgent desire to confess the truth to her, stopped only by the firm pressure of Drew's fingers on her own, almost as though he knew what was in her mind.

'Well, we'll see both of you at the countess's birthday party next weekend, and I'll give you a ring to let you know when I'm coming over, Holly,' Drew's mother told her as they walked across the car park.

Holly waited until she and Drew were safely inside the Range Rover before saying huskily, 'Drew, your mother thinks we're going to be married. I . . .'

'I know,' he told her, cutting off the rest of her sentence and looking briefly into her too pale face.

'I hate deceiving her like this,' Holly told him wretchedly. 'It seems so mean. Think how she's going to feel when she finds out.'

'That you're madly in love with someone else? Of course, you could always forget about Neston and marry me instead,' he told her whimsically.

Just for a moment her heart soared, and then across the car park she saw Howard, Rosamund and her parents, and it dropped again, making her ache inside with the force of her feeling.

'That isn't funny, Drew,' she told him in a tight little voice.

He started the engine, and must have reversed the vehicle with something less than his usual care, because it jerked a little.

'It wasn't meant to be,' he told her curtly, and once again she had the feeling that she had angered him, or maybe it was just that the sight of Rosamund with Howard had upset him.

By the time they got back the sun had gone and the sky was overcast, the wind bitingly cold.

'If the temperature keeps on dropping, we could have snow,' Drew announced laconically as he stopped the Range Rover.

'But we're only half-way through November,' Holly protested.

'It has been known. Don't you remember? We had snow in November during your last year at school.'

When she cast her mind back, she realised that they had, but how odd that Drew should remember it and she shouldn't.

'The school bus didn't make it, and I gave you and Rosamund a lift to school in my Land Rover.'

Oh, now she realised why!

CHAPTER NINE

DREW was right about the snow. The first few flakes fell three days later, just after his mother's visit to the farm.

Holly was well advanced with her work on the kitchen units now. She had dragged the outer panels in a soft shade of yellow over cream, wiping off the beading to make it stand out. Now she was painstakingly feathering *faux marbre* centre panels to each cupboard door. Later, if she felt so inclined, she would add her stencil.

Drew's mother had been flatteringly impressed, marvelling at the detailing and care she had taken, and announcing quite firmly that she was definitely going to commission Holly to work on her guest suite.

'The bedroom has fitted units and perhaps you could link them to the bathroom in some way, Holly. I'd rather like a blue and yellow colour scheme, I think. I've already got a fabric in mind.'

She had described it, and Holly, who'd recognised it as coming from a very popular traditional range, had known that she wouldn't have much problem in coming up with a couple of suitable colour schemes.

However, it had been as she was leaving that she had dropped her bombshell, announcing almost casually, 'I'm so pleased about you and Drew, my dear. I always have a large family gathering at

Christmas; normally Drew allows me to have it here because our small drawing-room simply isn't large enough. I want to make sure everyone comes this year so that they can meet you. I expect Drew will be giving you an engagement ring soon, and I want to plan something very special.'

What she was saying was virtually that she intended to hold an engagement party for them, Holly had recognised, and now she was sitting in the kitchen, wondering how on earth she was going to tell Drew, and watching the ever-increasing flakes of snow tumble down from the grey sky.

A commotion by the door disturbed her and she went to open it to let in the large tabby cat who was supposed to make her home in the stable, but who had attached herself to Holly. She had come to recognise the tabby's chirruping meouw.

The cat came in proudly and deposited a large fat mouse at her feet. Holly repressed the urge to scream, thankful to see that the poor thing was dead. The cat, plainly unaware of her feelings, wove its way round her legs, purring loudly, demanding praise for its cleverness. Holly petted it gingerly, wondering if she could persuade it to take its prey back outside.

Drew came in while she was standing there, his eyebrows lifting as he saw the mouse.

'You're honoured,' he told her wryly.

'Really?' Holly responded weakly, and then added in a voice that shook a little, 'Drew, how can I make her take it back outside?'

'You can't. Not without offending her. Tell her she's a wonderfully clever girl and pour her some milk.

With a bit of luck, while you're distracting her, I'll be able to dispose of it.'

It worked; while the cat drank her milk, Drew removed the small, furry corpse. He came back into the kitchen and washed his hands, eyeing her with concern as he saw her pale face.

'You're not frightened of mice, are you?' he asked her abruptly.

She shook her head. 'No, I know it's silly, but it just upset me . . . seeing the poor little thing.'

'Poor tender-hearted Holly,' he said drily, 'trying so desperately not to allow the giver to see how unwelcome the gift of love is.'

For some reason Holly felt as though the words held a meaning that eluded her. Perhaps it was because of the faint edge of bitterness that hardened his voice.

'Is it still snowing?' she asked him, changing the subject.

'Yes, and likely to continue to do so. I take it Mother came as planned?'

'Yes. Oh, Drew . . . the most dreadful thing . . . She intimated that she intends to give a Christmas party for us. She even hinted that she expects us to get engaged.'

He had been looking at her, watching the vivid play of emotions across her face, but now he turned away slightly, his voice muffled as he asked, 'What did you say to her?'

'Nothing. What could I say? I felt so awful for deceiving her.'

'Umm ... It might not be such a bad idea, you know. Getting engaged,' he said thoughtfully, as though he hadn't heard her last words. 'It might just be the incentive our laggard ex-partners need.'

'Oh, Drew, no!' Holly protested, her skin losing all its colour. How could she tell him that she couldn't bear the thought of pretending to be engaged to him? That she couldn't trust herself not to become so caught up in their self-created world of make-believe that she would never be able to leave it? 'No.'

For some reason he suddenly looked tired, and Holly realised guiltily that he must be feeling exactly the same way as she was herself.

'How could we?' she said huskily. 'I mean, when we both know that it wouldn't be real. I'd feel so guilty.'

'Would you? I thought any means was justified when love was at stake,' he said casually.

She had thought the same thing, too, once. But then she had been a heedless, naïve girl, with no awareness of what love was really all about.

'My family will be shocked,' he told her. 'After all, they're not sophisticated city folk, and you are living here with me. They'll expect you to make an honest man of me. I shall have to tell them that you're reverting to ancient custom and that you won't marry me until I've proved that I can give you a child.'

Holly's face flamed at his careless reference to an ancient custom among country folk that a couple did not marry until the bride had proved she could provide her groom with a son.

That had been important in the days when inheritance was a vital issue, but it wasn't embarrassment that was making her body tingle and her insides ache.

Holly had a bad dream that night. She dreamed that she was standing talking to Drew and suddenly a huge crowd of people swelled between them, parting them, and no matter how hard she struggled she couldn't get through the seething press of bodies to find him.

She called his name repeatedly, each call sharper and more frantic than the last, sobs tearing her chest and hurting her throat.

She came awake abruptly, shivering under the bedclothes, a tight, raw feeling in her throat that presaged tears. She wondered if she had actually cried or if it had only been part of her dream. What *was* real, though, was the aching feeling of despair that possessed her, the realisation that Drew was lost to her for ever.

Drew. She had known him for more than half her lifetime. Known him, liked him, and dismissed him as bucolic and unexciting, with a child's lack of depth of perception and wisdom, with a child's vain grasping for the ephemeral glitter of life. She had even, in her folly, scorned him a little and not found it strange that Rosamund should prefer Howard.

Now Howard was as a pale shadow, a flimsy, weak character whose very lack of any real substance when compared to Drew made her marvel that she had ever believed herself in love with him.

She was still shivering, her feet frozen beneath the duvet, and she knew it would be impossible for her to get back to sleep. She reached for her dressing-gown. She would go downstairs and sit in front of the Aga for a while, perhaps make herself a hot drink. She shivered again just thinking about it. Living in the city for so long, her body had lost its ability to adapt itself to changing temperatures, or perhaps the fault was hers for not armouring herself against them. In the same way she had neglected to armour herself against loving Drew.

The landing and the stairs creaked underfoot—comforting, solid sounds, the sounds of an old house that had known many lifetimes of joys and tears.

The cat was sitting by the range; she stretched and yawned, greeting Holly's entrance with soft, chirruping sounds of welcome as Holly switched on the lights.

Outside, the sky had cleared. The moon was sharp and bright, casting a coldly brilliant light. It danced off the rooftops of the cow sheds and barns with their frosting of snow. Holly went to the window to look outside. The yard was pristine white except for where the cat had walked.

How quickly and devastatingly winter could come to the land. Drew had planned to plough the last of the fields this week. Now that would have to wait until the ground thawed. He had explained to her how he was carefully channelling his resources into breeding and small high-profit crops, rather than the old-fashioned traditional mixed farming of his father's day: a dairy herd and grain crops.

She filled the kettle and switched it on. As she waited for it to boil she thought about Christmas and the party Drew's mother was planning. She thought about the kitchen and the woman who would eventually use it. Not her... Rosamund? If Drew had his way...

The kettle boiled. She reached for it through a haze of tears, sending the teapot crashing to the floor. The sound of it breaking seemed preternaturally loud. One sharp piece pierced her finger, making it bleed. She gave a low cry, and sucked it clean.

'Holly. What's wrong?'

She stared at Drew, his hair tousled, his chest bare as he tugged on his robe, his expression that of a man roused unexpectedly from a deep sleep.

The sight of him standing there made her react like a frightened child.

'I'm sorry, I've broken the teapot,' she said huskily, and then to her horror she started to cry.

Suddenly she was in Drew's arms, her head pressed into the warm curve of his shoulder, her sobs muffled by his robe. He was picking her up despite her muddled complaint about the mess on the floor and the danger to the cat. He paused to switch off the light and close the door, soothing her with soft words of comfort. Upstairs, he carried her to her room, frowning over its icy atmosphere.

'I opened the window,' Holly told him, 'and then I couldn't close it.'

'It's too cold for you to sleep in here. The temperature's dropped damn near ten degrees today. You can sleep in my room, and I'll use this one.'

'Drew, no.' But it was pointless to protest. He was already half-way there, shouldering open his door, and depositing her in a bed that was huge and blissfully warm.

'That better?' he asked her in an oddly husky voice as he released her, sitting on the side of the bed, and reaching out to brush a silky tangle of hair off her damp face.

She looked up at him, and her whole world seemed to turn over as she saw the look on his face.

Need...desire...urgency... All of them were there, darkening his skin with a hectic flush and drawing it tight against his cheekbones, dilating his eyes and turning them molten gold. In the space of a heartbeat he had turned from comforter to lover.

A startled protest rose to her lips and was checked as she trembled between the realistic, sensible cautioning of her head, and the heedless, helpless yearning of her heart.

'Drew, no,' she protested huskily. 'We *can't* just let our...our feelings for Howard and Rosamund trap us into a sort of sympathetic intimacy.'

She couldn't pretend that she didn't know what was in his mind...that she hadn't recognised, bone-deep and instinctively, despite her lack of experience, his sudden savage determination to make love to her.

'Does that mean that you don't want me?' he asked her huskily.

Not want him? The truth was there in her eyes for him to read. She heard him give a harsh groan of satisfaction, her eyes closing on a dizzying wave of response to him.

'No,' she heard herself saying shockingly. 'I want you very much. Oh, Drew, why do you make me say these things?'

'Perhaps because I'm very vulnerable. When a man is rejected sexually—and emotionally, when he's been aching for as long as I've been aching, Holly, it's a kind of sweet drug to him to know that he is, after all, desired. It makes him forget all kinds of things he should remember. It makes him... Oh, God, Holly, you feel so good in my arms. You know I want to make love to you, don't you?'

Of course she did. She had known it from the moment he looked at her, and wantonly her heart had leapt in joyous response to it.

'Drew, I'm not Rosamund,' she reminded him, forced by her conscience to do so. 'You know I'm not experienced, or...' She flushed wildly and admitted honestly, 'This will be the first time I've made love. Howard——'

'Forget Howard,' he told her curtly. 'I promise I'll make it good for you, Holly.'

'Just like in the books?' she said lightly, trying to hold on to reality.

'Better,' Drew promised her. 'Much, much better. Let me show you...'

It was all wrong. He didn't love her, she knew that, but she loved him and her body ached for him, and there was a certain odd inevitability to what was happening between them, almost as though it was in some way pre-ordained; almost as though she had been slowly moving toward this moment all of her life.

Now that she had reached it there were no doubts, no fears, no second thoughts, only a pure, clear joy that there should be this time, this togetherness, this man. Because, even without love, Drew would give her pleasure, consideration, compassion and respect, and she would give him . . .

What would she give him? she wondered hazily as he touched her. The full outpouring of her love, some small surcease, some small touch of balm against his hurts? And perhaps a memory that he would cherish in a tiny corner of his heart.

'If I do anything that hurts or offends you, Holly, please tell me,' he whispered against her mouth, adding huskily, 'And you *will* have to tell me because I ache so damn much inside I can't be sure I'm capable of recognising anything else.' He saw her eyes widen and smiled mirthlessly. 'Have I frightened you? Join the club. I'm beginning to frighten myself.' He took her hand and placed it against his heart. It slammed against her palm heavily and far too fast. His skin felt moist and hot, and the delicate abrasion of his body hair against her fingertips made her tremble painfully. And yet she couldn't stop herself from caressing him tentatively, from stroking his hot flesh and feeling her own heartbeat pick up the shallow, frantic rhythm of his as his muscles tensed. His hand cupped her jaw, holding her mouth under his own while he tasted it, tormented it, and finally opened it with a muted violence that sent a wild thrill of dazed pleasure through her body and made her breasts peak and harden and her stomach melt.

She reached up and clasped her hands behind Drew's neck, her fingertips lost in the thick silkiness of his hair. The pressure of his mouth altered, softening, coaxing, suborning her will-power to the strong tide of his desire.

Instincts she had not known she possessed guided her, her body pliant, fluid, conspiring with his to ensure that she couldn't resist the slow, drugging force of her own need. Her nails dug tenderly into Drew's flesh and he made a sound of pleasure deep in his throat, lifting his mouth from hers to stare at her with desire-drugged, brilliant eyes. Dark colour burned his cheekbones, and she touched him tentatively, delicately absorbing the heat into her fingertips.

His heart slammed against his ribs and her eyes widened in shocked recognition of her own effect on him. She saw his mouth curl in brief acknowledgement of his own weakness, and in her veins the heady drug of sexual power sang its siren song.

She cupped his face, as he had done hers, letting her flesh absorb the hard imprint of his, feeling the sharp stubble of his beard against her palm, sliding her hand downwards until it rested against his throat. She felt the muscles there convulse, and the knowledge that he wanted her fed her own desire.

Drew caught hold of her hand, lifting it to his mouth, licking the soft pads at the base of her fingers, nibbling her sensitised flesh, making her heart turn over inside her body and her muscles go weak as he punished her for tormenting him.

He moved, his weight pressing her body deeper into the bed, and even through the thickness of her nightshirt and robe her breasts responded to the heat and proximity of him.

This was still new to her, this aching tenderness that fed her imagination with wanton desires, that made her long to feel the intimate touch of his flesh against her own.

'Let me see you, Holly. Let me touch you,' Drew begged against her lips, his voice low and slurred like that of a man hopelessly caught up in something beyond his control. It pleased her that she could make him feel like this, react like this, and her spine arched with delicate pride as he removed her clothes, her senses glorying in the wonder and raw desire she saw in his face as he gazed down at her.

His hand trembled as he traced the delicate line of her collarbone and then slid along the outer curve of her breast, his thumb almost brushing the dark aureole of flesh that crowned it, before his hand tightened over the narrow span of her ribcage, his fingers biting almost painfully into her flesh.

Eyes the colour of dark fire locked on her own, the message she read there making her stomach kick in wild excitement. His hand tensed beneath the soft swell of her breast, and, as though he had asked her, she said, 'Yes. Yes, Drew,' and to her own amazement took his hand and placed it against her breast, breathing in sharply as she saw the fierce desire flood his face and felt his fingers tighten around her. And then he was caressing her, touching, stroking, teaching her things about her own body she had never dreamed existed. The world spun dizzily around her and she closed her eyes, opened them abruptly seconds later as she felt the heat of Drew's mouth against her flesh.

She drew in ragged breaths of delirious pleasure. How had he known of her need to have him caress her just like that, to feel the heat of his mouth drag against the swollen peaks of her breast in exactly that way, to...? She cried out incoherently as he drew fiercely on her nipple, and her womb convulsed in tiny, shimmering waves of pleasure.

'Holly. Holly...'

When had he removed his own clothes? she wondered confusedly as he pressed hot, fierce kisses on her throat and face, and she felt the hard arousal of him against her.

It felt so right, this heat and weight, her body adapting itself to it instinctively, so instinctively, in fact, that Drew tensed momentarily as her thighs parted to accommodate him, her body in its innocence eagerly responding to the arousal of his.

He had wanted this for so long...ached for it, yearned for it, and yet now... Now he knew that he couldn't take her without telling her.

Holly felt his tension and opened her eyes, every instinct she possessed screaming against the impossible. Drew had changed his mind. He didn't want her. She could feel it in the sudden coolness of his skin, that tension in his muscles.

'Holly,' he began unsteadily, and she knew that he was going to tell her that they must stop, that...

She wouldn't let it happen. She wouldn't let him reject her. She would show him that she could give him just as much satisfaction as Rosamund, and far,

far more love. Reaching up, she sealed his mouth with her fingertips, her eyes glowing brilliantly in her small face.

'Please don't stop, Drew,' she whispered huskily. 'Not now... Not now...' And then she covered his throat and chest with pleading, open-mouthed kisses that made him groan out loud and which brought the hectic flush of heat to his skin, his body making its own unmistakable response to her plea.

She had won. He wouldn't reject her now. He couldn't, and her body rejoiced in its female power as she gladly let him take control of her shuddering flesh and make it his own.

There was pain briefly, and it made them both tense, and then as it faded Holly moved. As though the enticement of her was more than he could resist, Drew gave in to the urgings of his own need.

As his mouth silenced her soft little cries of pleasure, the words of love he knew he could not utter filled his soul. She was his... if only briefly, and he would show her how much he cherished the gift she was giving him.

Later... looking back with the sophistication of experience, Holly recognised how difficult it must have been for Drew to control his desire to match the pace of her own inexperience. The sensation of him moving within her delighted her emergent senses, making her respond frantically to each powerful thrust until he held her and showed her how to match his pulsing rhythm so that their bodies moved in fierce accord.

She felt the striving, the aching need to reach some totally necessary goal without knowing what it was, only that the driving force of Drew's body was a piper's call to which her own must respond, and the first quivers of climactic pleasure caught her by surprise, tensing her body, so that at first Drew thought he had hurt her. But when she opened her eyes and he saw the dawning of what was happening to her mirrored there, he whispered urgently, 'Relax, Holly. Let it happen. Don't fight it.'

And, as her muscles relaxed in obedience, he felt for himself the delicious, frantic little convulsions, and coaxed them and nurtured them until the soft body beneath his writhed and twisted in elemental pleasure and Holly cried out to him, begging him for release.

Her nails scored his back, her mouth pressing hot, urgent kisses against his skin, and, as the surges of pleasure grew quickly more and more urgent, Holly felt his own control snap, and knew that he had joined her in that magical place where nothing existed save for the sweet culmination they both sought.

They found it together: the ripples of pleasure exploding inside her so that she cried out and clung to Drew, feeling the shudders that racked him, the fierce tension that held him, and then the hot release of his flesh deep within her own. A rare, precious moment of communion that she knew she would treasure for the rest of her life.

Later, when he had eased himself from her body and tucked them both beneath the comfort of the duvet, she slept curled against him, replete with physical and emotional satisfaction, warmed by the hard bulk of his body, protected by the arm he curled round her, imprisoned by the firm weight of his leg across her thighs.

As she drifted deep into sleep, she thought she felt his soft breath stir her hair as he whispered in her ear, 'I love you, Holly. I love you.'

But she knew it was only wishful thinking, because locked away deep in her heart was the knowledge that he loved Rosamund.

CHAPTER TEN

HOLLY woke up slowly, like someone surfacing from a very deep ocean. Her body ached pleasurably and felt different. Tiny, darting thoughts battered against her drowsy mind, demanding admittance: sharp thorns of a pain she didn't want to admit.

She opened her eyes, huge and dazed still, her skin softly pink with warmth, her dark hair silkily soft.

As she opened her eyes, she wondered why Drew was sitting on the side of her bed, watching her so gravely. He looked as though he had a lot on his mind. His face looked oddly drawn and grim. Outside, the sun was shining, glinting off the snow-capped roofs of the buildings, but surely not the buildings she normally saw through her window.

'Drew...' she began uncertainly, and then, as if someone were ripping a shroud from a coffin, everything came flooding back. Her skin burned, her eyes dilating with knowledge. Drew reached out to touch her, but she shrank back—not from him, but from herself.

'Holly,' Drew said quietly, 'we have to talk. Last night...'

'Oh, Drew, no! I don't want to... I know how you feel,' she told him in a low voice, avoiding his glance. 'And I know I should never have allowed what happened last night to happen.'

'I see.' She sensed the distance in him immediately, and was confused by it. She thought he would have been reassured to hear she was behaving so sensibly. She had been about to tell him that she had no regrets, that she knew that he loved Rosamund, but she felt his weight leave the bed, and knew that he was walking away from her.

'I expect you'll want me to leave,' she added huskily. 'I'll pack my things this morning.'

'Leave?' He strode back to the bed, frowning down at her as she turned to look at him. Two hectic spots of colour burned his cheeks. 'Oh, no, Holly, you're not going to do that,' he told her flatly, adding emotionlessly, 'We made a bargain, remember?'

She moistened her dry lips with the tip of her tongue, and wished she hadn't as she saw Drew looking at her, and her stomach muscles contracted on a wave of remembered pleasure that made her go weak and dizzy.

She wanted him! She wanted him, right now, this minute. She wanted him to take her in his arms and kiss her and caress her as he had done last night. She wanted to feel the hot pulse of his flesh within her own, easing that tight, aching sensation that was even now possessing her.

Frantically, she looked away from him. 'I didn't think you'd want me to stay.'

'In case I'm tempted to make love to you again?' he demanded harshly.

Make love to her again . . . Her body grew hot and she had to force herself not to look at him and let him see the need in her eyes. She could feel the anger emanating from him, and acknowledged that he had every right to it. She was the one who had insisted, she was the one who had begged him not to stop. Of course, he knew that wasn't why she wanted to leave.

'If I give you my word that I won't touch you again, will you stay, Holly? At least until after the countess's birthday party.'

She clung gratefully to the opportunity to stay with him, even while part of her mind despised her for it.

'If that's what you want . . .'

'What I want?' he exclaimed savagely. 'What I want, Holly, is . . .' He saw her go white and broke off, muttering something under his breath. 'I'll leave you to get dressed. I'll be out for most of the day. We could have more snow, and I'll have to organise feed for the sheep.'

Drew had a very small flock of prize wool-giving sheep that grazed on the less fertile acreage of the farm. 'I shan't be back until late, Holly. I'm relying on you to keep your word,' he told her quietly, and then added wryly, 'Think how it's going to look for me if I manage to lose two girlfriends in such a short space of time . . .'

'I won't leave,' she promised him solemnly, and for a moment, as he hesitated, she had the impression that he wanted to come over and kiss her. If he did, he managed to resist the impulse, heading instead for the door.

After he had gone she got up. She and Drew were lovers! Her skin shivered in remembered pleasure, the faint bruises she saw forming on her pale flesh reminding her of the intensity of Drew's passion. And that passion had been for her, not for Rosamund. He had wanted *her*...caressed *her*...kissed *her*...made love to *her*...and she would have the joy of that knowledge with her for always, even though she would not have Drew.

It was hard to behave as though nothing had changed, but she knew that she must. She must not burden Drew with her love. She must be as sophisticated as Rosamund would be in the same situation. She must just accept what had been and acknowledge that it could never be again. It would be hard, harder than it had been before. Sighing, she went downstairs and made herself some breakfast. Then, when she had cleared her things away, she set to work on her stencil. The work needed concentration and care, and helped her to get her life back into its normal perspective.

Her tummy told her when it was lunch time, and she stopped what she was doing to heat some of the soup she had made the previous day. In London she would simply have bought a can, but here in the country that seemed a crime. Her mother was a very domesticated woman, and she had taught Holly all her skills. Was it only yesterday lunch time that Drew had praised her, claiming that the soup was even better than his mother's?

Would she ever feel totally at ease with him again? Would she ever be able to look at him without remembering the feel and scent of his skin, the power of his body, the vulnerability of his need? Her body contracted on a fresh wave of desire, and she stared blindly out of the window, watching fresh flakes of snow drift earthwards.

She was just ladling the soup into a bowl when she saw Drew drive into the yard. Her heart leapt and thudded against her chest wall, nervous excitement making her go weak with pleasure.

He came in, brushing snowflakes off his jacket.

'I thought you weren't coming in for lunch.'

'I changed my mind,' he told her grimly.

Despite the healthy glow of his skin, he looked tired and drawn still. Had he come back to check that she had kept her promise?

'I wont leave, Drew,' she told him gently. 'Not until you ask me to.'

An odd look crossed his face. He came up to her, his hand on her throat, his eyes gravely serious as he warned her, 'Be careful what promises you make to me, Holly. It could be that I will never ask that!'

Just for a moment she let herself believe that this was real and not just a misplaced piece of gallantry on Drew's part. She closed her eyes and only opened them again when she had the strength of will to say firmly, 'Drew, there's Rosamund and——'

'And Howard,' he interrupted before she could go on. 'Well, at least he won't be able to accuse you of being inexperienced now,' he told her with grim cruelty, watching the colour come and go in her face. 'Is that why you made love with me last night, Holly? Because you thought it would make Howard...'

'No...no...you know it wasn't,' she contradicted him sharply, her pain showing in her eyes. 'Drew, how could you believe that?'

She heard him groan and then she was in his arms, his heart thudding wildly against her. 'I'm sorry,

Holly. God, I'm sorry,' she heard him mutter as he shaped her skull and then tilted her head so that his mouth could whisper the apologies against her own, and finally he kissed her deeply, hungrily, like a man starving for the sensation of her mouth against his own.

When he released her, his face was white.

'Perhaps you're right,' he said quietly. 'Perhaps you should.' His thumb touched the bruised fullness of her lips. 'But not yet, Holly. Not until after the countess's party. We'll talk about it then. All right?'

She nodded, too shaken to speak. Why had he kissed her like that? she wondered when he had gone. Because he had sensed her need, because he had wanted to comfort her, to apologise? But it had been a kiss of passion, not apology, and she had felt the unmistakable leap of his flesh, the urgent arousal of his body against her own, and had known that he shared the desire shimmering through her.

Perhaps the Bible was right, and the apple of desire was a fruit that, once tasted, could not easily be put aside, even when that desire was not allied to love.

Why was he insisting that she stay until after the countess's party? To give him time to prepare a story for his mother? So that they could have one last attempt at breaking Rosamund and Howard's engagement? But Howard wouldn't be there.

Rosamund would, though, and perhaps he was hoping that, being alone, seeing him with someone else would fuel her jealousy to such a pitch that she decided it was Drew she preferred. Certainly she was showing a good deal more interest in her old love than

Howard was in his, but she didn't care. The last thing she wanted right now was Howard. The only thing she wanted was Drew . . . the one thing she could not have.

For the rest of the week Drew seemed to be avoiding her, working long hours outside, coming in exhausted, to retire to his office after they had eaten, claiming that he had paperwork to catch up on.

Holly didn't press for his company; she could see the lines of tension scored alongside his mouth, see the tightening of flesh over bones that suddenly seemed almost too prominent.

She, too, turned to her work for escape, diligently concentrating on applying the delicate stencil to the painted cupboard doors. As she filled in the outline of the pretty, fresh green leaves, she tried not to imagine Rosamund working in this kitchen, using these cupboards that Drew had built so well.

Only that morning she had spoken on the phone to Jan, telling her that so far Nantwich looked the most likely venue for the new shop. Jan had been so enthusiastic that she hadn't felt able to tell her of her own reluctance to proceed with their plans. Was it really wise of her to allow herself to remain so close to Drew? Wouldn't it be more sensible to return just as soon as she could to London?

But careerwise there would never be another opportunity like this one, and she was going to need her career, she admitted grimly; because she knew now that she would never marry, never have a child without Drew.

In today's post had come a sheaf of details from local estate agents of various shop properties in the three areas they had investigated. One in particular in Nantwich had caught her eye: a rather neglected, double-fronted shop property with a spacious flat above it, and, even better, a generous garden behind it.

The price was within the limits she and Jan had discussed, and Jan had urged her to make further investigations. Her car was outside, she could drive to Nantwich quite easily if she wished, and arrange to view the property, but once she did that she would have taken the first step in committing herself to staying within Drew's orbit. To condemning herself to a life of living in proximity to a man she loved and could never have. So instead she concentrated on her stencil, trying to hold back time and the decision she had to make.

She would do it after the countess's party, she told herself, after she and Drew had discussed what they were going to do, how they were going to end their supposed relationship, because she was quite sure that was what Drew had on his mind. One last-ditch attempt to convince Rosamund that he was the one she loved, and, whatever the outcome, their plan was finished with.

Holly had a dim memory of her parents attending the countess's famous parties, and recollected that a gift of some sort had been *de rigueur*. She mentioned it to Drew when he came in. She saw that he was looking at the pile of estate agents' papers on the table and said uncertainly, 'They came this morning.

There's one in Nantwich that sounds ideal. Jan wants me to go and view it . . .'

'When are you going?' he asked her, frowning, as though his thoughts were really elsewhere.

Probably on Rosamund and how difficult it could be if she decided to remain in the area once he and Rosamund were back together. Holly was sure he must be bitterly regretting making love to her, but she couldn't find the words to tell him that any fears he had of her revealing what had happened to Rosamund were groundless. No matter what the provocation, she could never sully her very precious memories by using them in a vindictive kind of way. It simply wasn't in her nature, and it hurt that he shouldn't know this without having to be told.

'After . . . after the countess's party,' she told him quietly, and watched as he gave her a quick look.

His frown lightened as he questioned, 'So you're still considering going ahead with the partnership . . . with staying in the area?'

Why should he look and sound so pleased? It ran completely contrary to her own anguished thoughts, and for a moment she could only stare at him.

'Er—yes,' she managed to answer at last. 'Yes, I am. It's far too good a career opportunity to give up,' she added in a husky voice, so that he didn't think it was because of him, because she was cherishing any foolish and impossible dreams.

'What about Howard? If he drops Rosamund, it's unlikely that her father will keep him on.'

For a moment her face was blank, as though she was having great difficulty in remembering who Howard was, and then it cleared.

She almost told him that she couldn't care less what Howard did, and that, moreover, she doubted that he would ever consider giving up a wealthy bride like Rosamund for someone like her. Then she reminded herself that, although the scales had fallen from her eyes, they still blinded Drew, and he would not want to hear that she believed that Rosamund and Howard were perfect for one another, both being equally self-obsessed and selfish.

'I'll cross that bridge if and when I come to it,' she contented herself with saying lightly, before returning to her original question about what she could get the countess as a birthday gift.

'She had a collection of antique button hooks,' Drew told her. 'I know a place in Chester that sells them. We could have lunch at the Grosvenor on Saturday and buy her a present at the same time.'

It made her dizzy to think that he actually wanted to spend time with her. All week he seemed to have been avoiding her, and now here he was casually suggesting that they spend almost all day together.

'If you're sure you don't mind. I know you've been busy——' she began breathlessly.

As he turned away from her she thought she heard him mutter under his breath, 'Yes, busy trying to stop myself from thinking about how you felt in my arms.'

But the words were husky and low-toned, and she suspected she must have imagined them, conjuring them up out of her own reckless love.

* * *

By Saturday the snow had gone, but the morning dawned clear and sharp with frost and a bright November day.

Holly were her red dress again and her black coat, knowing that the colours suited her. Drew was wearing the blouson she had chosen, and as she crossed the farmyard with him she ached to be free to tell him how masculine and desirable he looked.

New clothes hadn't changed the man he was—they couldn't—but they had underlined the special maleness of him, and her heart thumped precariously as she watched him move, lean and long-limbed and very, very much a man.

Chester was busy, packed with pre-Christmas shoppers, but Holly liked the busy atmosphere, the sense of community, the familiarity of the Cheshire accent mingling with the drawled vowels of Chester's wealthy county set. She felt at home here, comfortable and at ease.

She laughed as she watched a group of children standing in front of a tumbling clown. Musicians played on the corners of the streets, cheerful, smiling students with placards proclaiming their musical status. It was an innovative way for students to earn extra money, and the crowds seemed to like it, being generous with the silver they dropped into the upturned hat.

Christmas. A feeling of melancholy suddenly struck her. Where would she be then? Back in London in her lonely flat? Last year she had spent Christmas with Jan. They would invite her to join them again this year, but she still did not feel entirely at ease with their sophisticated crowd. If she had the money and the time, she could fly out to her brother and parents. They would welcome her.

Given free choice, though, there was only one place she wanted to be, one person she wanted to spend such an evocative and emotional season with.

Drew.

She looked up at him, and caught him watching her with a sombre expression.

'Don't,' he said rawly, and her throat closed with tears. Had he read the love in her eyes and warned her not to betray it? For both their sakes? But she realised she was wrong when he added, 'He isn't worth it, Holly. He isn't worth a single one of your tears, damn him,' he added gruffly, and to her astonishment he took hold of her in the middle of the crowded street and held her in his arms, hugging her briefly, his mouth tender against the closed corners of her eyes.

She could have stayed there for ever, and would have done if a crowd of laughing teenagers hadn't forced them apart.

'We ought to go and find the countess's present,' she told Drew.

'Yes. Come on, this way.'

The small antique shop was packed with treasures, and on a different occasion Holly could have quite happily spent the rest of the day browsing there.

The owner had a good selection of hooks to show them, and in the end they bought two that formed a pair. Watching them being packed away in a worn case, Holly couldn't help wondering where she would be the next time the countess had a birthday. Not with Drew. Never again with Drew . . .

The Grosvenor was packed, but Holly was glad; its busyness stopped her from brooding and made it impossible for them to have any kind of personal conversation.

They left after they had had lunch, Holly shaking her head when Drew asked her if she would like to call on his mother and stepfather. The day had been enough of a strain without adding that. What would Drew tell his mother? The truth? That they had played a game out of innocence and love, not meaning to hurt or wound, not meaning to deceive? Holly hoped his mother would understand. She rather suspected that she might.

When they got back, Drew left to check on the stock. Holly made a pot of tea, wrapped the countess's present in the pretty paper they had bought, and wrote out the card that Drew had insisted was to come from both of them. She looked at their names and had to bite down hard on her bottom lip to stop herself from bursting into tears.

Drew had already warned her that the countess was inclined to be parsimonious, and that the antiquated central-heating system of Elsworth Park was not inclined to be efficient, and so she wore a new wool dress in steel-grey, its plainness relieved by the sparkle of rhinestones across the shoulders and down the sleeves.

The dress was short and cut to skim her curves flatteringly. With it she wore fine, dark grey silk tights and her one and only pair of good high-heeled evening shoes.

The black velvet coat she had worn that afternoon was the only one she had that was suitable to wear over the dress, and she acknowledged a little despondently as she studied her reflection that her dress, with its neat, high collar and long sleeves, was hardly likely to excite male desire.

However, when she went downstairs Drew looked at her for a long time in silence in a way that made her heart flutter until she told herself that she was being stupid.

Drew himself looked vigorously attractive in his evening clothes, and she could only marvel that she had ever compared him unfavourably to Howard. There was something subtle and enticing about the hard play of muscles beneath the matt fabric. She wanted to go up to him and touch him.

Quickly quelling the impulse, she gave him an over-bright smile and picked up the countess's present.

'Ready?' he asked her.

Silently, she nodded.

Elsworth Park had been built in the late eighteenth century by an eccentric millionaire ancestor of the countess's, who, it was rumoured, had inherited his wealth from a slave-trading uncle in the West Indies. Whether or not this was true, it was a story that was often repeated with relish and embellishment locally, even by the countess herself, who rather enjoyed her family's aristocratic eccentricity.

She was receiving her guests in some state in what had once been the drawing-room. Holly found the combination of so much faded magenta silk and gilt rather overpowering, but there was no denying the beauty of the Savonnaire rug that covered the floor.

The countess received her graciously, recollecting her parents with apparent ease, but her real warmth was reserved for Drew, whom she greeted in very much the manner of an eighteenth-century beauty with a favoured courtier.

Watching Drew with her, Holly could only applaud both his tact and his kindness. She herself moved discreetly to one side, tensing when she heard Rosamund's familiar voice at her elbow.

The other girl was wearing a vivid blue puffball dress that exposed her tanned arms and shoulders and revealed the upper swell of her breasts. Privately Holly thought the colour too strong for her, but there was no denying the expensive exclusivity of the pure silk dress. Rosamund was wearing satin shoes dyed to match, and she studied Holly's own plain grey outfit with barely concealed contempt.

'Didn't Drew warn you that this was a formal "do"?' she taunted her cattily.

Holly didn't allow herself to respond. What was the point?

'God, why on earth doesn't he tell the old bat to get lost?' she commented viciously, watching the countess flirt outrageously with Drew.

'Perhaps because he doesn't want to hurt her feelings,' Holly responded with dignity.

'He won't marry you, you know,' Rosamund added conversationally. 'Take my advice ... go back to London before it's too late and you make a complete fool of yourself. Who knows,' she added carelessly, 'you might even be able to persuade Howard to take you back.'

'Howard? But he's engaged to you,' Holly protested.

'Not any more,' Rosamund told her, and, seeing the predatory way her glance settled on Drew's broad shoulders, Holly's heart sank. Without saying the words, Rosamund was letting her know that she considered Drew to be her very private property and that she fully intended to reclaim him.

She permitted herself one tiny dig, keeping her head held high as she said quietly, 'You surprise me. I should have thought the two of you were ideally suited.'

Rosamund stared at her, her pale blue eyes like chips of ice.

'Drew is mine,' she told her flatly, and Holly actually took a step backwards, so vicious was the look she gave her. 'Mine,' Rosamund reiterated, 'and no one, least of all a simpering little fool like you, is going to take him away from me.'

Without another word, she turned on her heel and walked up to Drew, linking her arm through his, almost dragging him away from the countess. Holly stood and watched them, unable to do or say anything.

Their plan had worked ... but with what bitter consequences for her! She suspected that she was going to have to resign herself to being a wallflower for the rest of the evening, but to her astonishment Drew returned within five minutes.

'Why didn't you say you weren't feeling well?' he exclaimed.

'What?'

'Rosamund just told me that you weren't feeling well and that you'd said you wanted to leave.'

'I . . .'

Rosamund had told him *that*?

She was still wondering why when Rosamund herself came toward them, tucking a proprietorial arm through Drew's as she said to Holly with insincerity, 'Oh, you're still here, then. Look, why don't I get Dad's chauffeur to run you back to the farm? You look terrible. So pale . . .'

No doubt she did in contrast to Rosamund's glowing tan, Holly acknowledged grimly.

'There's no need for that,' Drew said quietly, disengaging himself. 'I'll take Holly home.'

'Oh, Drew, no! There's no need for you to leave. I'm sure Holly doesn't want to spoil your evening. In fact, I suspect she's looking forward to making a sneaky phone call to Howard,' she added archly. 'Our engagement's off. And if Holly's anything like as crazy about Howard as he said, then she must be desperately anxious to speak to him. They do say the best way to catch a man is on the rebound, don't they?' she added with a tiny laugh that jarred on Holly's nerves. And suddenly, she did feel very sick indeed.

She swayed where she stood, hating Rosamund with an intensity she had never experienced in her life, not even when she had thought she had stolen Howard from him.

She heard Drew saying quietly, 'I think you've said enough, Rosamund,' and then, above her shrill protests, adding, 'I'm taking Holly home.'

'The countess,' Holly whispered, as he put his arm around her and guided her towards the door.

'She'll understand. I'll telephone and explain tomorrow.'

Outside, in the cold night air, Holly breathed deeply, trying to stop the shudders wrenching her apart inside.

Drew didn't say a word during the drive back, but she could sense the tension in him and knew that he must be bitterly disappointed at hating to leave Rosamund. Not that he had anything to worry about. The other woman had made it more than plain how she felt about him.

These thoughts much to the forefront of her mind as Drew unlocked the kitchen door, she said tiredly, 'Well, at least our plan worked. Rosamund wants you back, Drew. She told me as much earlier. You must want to get back to her. It was good of you to bring me home, but there's no need to stay...'

'No need? Is it true, Holly?' he demanded harshly. 'Do you want to get me out of the way so that you can plead with Neston to take you back?'

'No.'

Real revulsion thickened her voice, and before she could stop herself she felt the tears press hotly against her eyes and slide relentlessly down her face.

'Oh, God, Holly! I'm sorry, I didn't mean to upset you.'

He came toward her and Holly knew that he was going to take hold of her. Desperately she backed away, and begged, 'No, Drew, please don't touch me.'

He went stock still and stared at her, his face suddenly as pale as her own, and then abruptly it burned with dark colour.

'I see,' he said stiffly. 'Of course, I should have realised how you'd feel. I suppose you think you can't go back to Neston because of what happened with me... because we made love. God dammit, Holly, doesn't the fact that we did, and you and he *never* did, tell you anything?' he demanded explosively.

'Yes,' she said woodenly. 'It tells me that you're a very sensual man, desperately missing the woman you love, and that I'm...' And then her voice became totally suspended as her throat locked.

'And that you're what, Holly?' Drew demanded thickly, ignoring her earlier plea and taking her into his arms. 'Sorry that you can't love me the way I love you? Sorry that you made love with me? Sorry that...'

Within his arms, Holly tensed and then demanded tearfully, 'Say that again.'

'Say what again?'

'That you love me!'

He hesitated and then said quietly, 'Didn't you already know it? Everyone else does.'

'No... I thought you loved Rosamund.'

'After the way I made love to *you*?' he demanded drily. 'Holly, I've never loved Rosamund. She's an avaricious, scheming, stupid woman, and besides, how could I possibly love her when I've always loved you?'

'Always?' she whispered, her eyes enormous.

'Since you were sixteen,' he whispered back, bending to capture the tremor of her mouth as though he couldn't resist its temptation.

Holly made an incoherent sound, and then subsided into his arms. It was a long time before he released her.

'You really thought I loved Rosamund?' he demanded wonderingly.

'You let me think so. You told me she'd broken your heart,' Holly reminded him accusingly.

'No. You assumed she had, and I . . . well, it was the most attention you'd paid me in over five years, and I wasn't going to spoil it by telling you I wasn't sharing your misery. And then fate seemed to hand me a golden opportunity. When you suggested that we pretend to have fallen in love, I could hardly believe my good luck. I told myself if I couldn't make you forget Neston, then I didn't deserve you. *Have* I made you forget him?' he asked her softly.

'Almost from the very start,' Holly admitted shyly. 'When I bumped into him in Knutsford, I couldn't imagine what I'd ever seen in him. He seemed such a pale shadow of a man in comparison to you. But Rosamund told me she wanted you back,' she added quietly. 'She . . .'

'Rosamund is an opportunist. She's wanted me for years, Holly,' he told her frankly, 'in much the same way she's wanted a new car or a fur coat. I've never wanted her, but she's an expert at refusing to see what she doesn't want to see. I suspect she broke with Howard hoping that you would go back to him and that would leave her in a position to comfort me. In fact, I suspect she had much the same thoughts in her mind as I had when you wept broken-heartedly over me for that idiot, Neston. When you were sixteen I looked at you and knew I loved you, but you were still a child and I was a very poor young man with no future to offer any woman. The years went by; I only saw you occasionally when you came home. We'd chat and you were pleasant and friendly, but I knew you just didn't see me as a man. I told myself I'd get over you, and then, as though fate had decided to intercede on my behalf, you came home.'

'And the night we made love?' Holly whispered.

'I couldn't help myself,' he said simply. 'I'd wanted you too much for too long. It was like falling off a cliff, once I'd taken that first fatal step, there was no going back.'

'I can't quite believe it all,' Holly told him shakily. 'It's almost as though I've walked into a magical dream.'

'Shock tends to have that effect,' Drew agreed. 'I feel much the same way myself. Of course, we could soon prove whether we're dreaming or not, I suppose, by sticking pins in one another—or we could simply forget about the pins, and go on dreaming together.'

Holly looked up at him and said quietly, 'Yes... Yes, I'd like that, Drew. Just so long as when I wake up in the morning, you're there beside me.'

She saw the look of love and need transform his face, and her breath caught in her throat. It was true, he did love her; the only wonder was that she had not realised it before.

'For the rest of our lives,' Drew told her solemnly. And then he lifted her left hand to his mouth and kissed her ring finger.

'Write to your parents, Holly. Ask them to come home as soon as they can. I've waited patiently since you were sixteen, and suddenly I'm finding I can't be patient any more. My mother's right,' he added huskily, 'you'd be a beautiful winter bride.'

And she was, and as a wedding present, her new husband gave her the keys for the shop in Nantwich.

'Two new partners in one week,' she teased breathlessly as they left on their honeymoon. 'You and Jan.' And, although he scowled at her, she knew that Drew would always encourage and support her in whatever she chose to do. The shop was the icing on the cake, but Drew was the cake itself, and the meat and drink of her life, and he always would be.

Harlequin Presents

Coming Next Month

#1287 BELONGING Sally Cook
Mandy always knew she was adopted, but having grown up so different from her adoptive parents, she decides to trace her real mother. While her search is successful, she finds the attractive Grant Livingstone is highly suspicious of her motives.

#1288 THE ULTIMATE CHOICE Emma Darcy
According to Kelly, the new owner of Marian Park is an arrogant swine who betrayed her grandfather and who wants to ruin Kelly's show-jumping career. Determined not to be stopped, she confronts Justin St. John, with all guns blazing....

#1289 TAKING CHANCES Vanessa Grant
It seems an odd request even for Misty's detective agency. Why does Zeb Turner want her to kidnap him? Finding out, Misty lands herself with more than she'd bargained for—maybe even more than she can cope with!

#1290 RUNAWAY WIFE Charlotte Lamb
Francesca has everything, so it seems—Oliver, her handsome, successful husband; a healthy son; and a lovely home. She believes she's merely a symbol of his success to Oliver and needs and wants—far more than that from life.

#1291 THE SEDUCTION OF SARA Joanna Mansell
Sara isn't too pleased to have Lucas Farraday following her around Peru. She thinks he's just a penniless drifter. Gradually she relaxes and gets used to his presence and his help. And that's when Lucas makes his next move.

#1292 RECKLESS HEART Kate Proctor
Ever since Sian McAllister's new boss, Nicholas Sinclair, had jumped to the wrong conclusions about her, life has been difficult. And the situation becomes impossible when Sian realizes that despite their strong disagreements, she's falling in love with him.

#1293 GENTLE DECEPTION Frances Roding
Rosy's love for her married cousin, Elliott, is entirely platonic, but not everyone sees it that way. To prove them wrong, Rosy has to find herself a man. Callum Blake is perfectly willing to be her pretend lover—yet what if pretence becomes reality?

#1294 DESIGNED WITH LOVE Kathryn Ross
Drew Sheldon is Amanda's ex-fiancé—and when her father sells the family firm to him, Amanda has a problem. She needs her job, but can she live with the power Drew now holds over her when she has an idea he really might want revenge?

Available in August wherever paperback books are sold, or through Harlequin Reader Service:

In the U.S.
901 Fuhrmann Blvd.
P.O. Box 1397
Buffalo, N.Y. 14240-1397

In Canada
P.O. Box 603
Fort Erie, Ontario
L2A 5X3

THE LOVES OF A CENTURY...

Join American Romance in a nostalgic look back at the Twentieth Century—at the lives and loves of American men and women from the turn-of-the-century to the dawn of the year 2000.

Journey through the decades from the dance halls of the 1900s to the discos of the seventies ... from Glenn Miller to the Beatles ... from Valentino to Newman ... from corset to miniskirt ... from beau to Significant Other.

Relive the moments ... recapture the memories.

Look now for the CENTURY OF AMERICAN ROMANCE series in Harlequin American Romance. In one of the four American Romance titles appearing each month, for the next twelve months, we'll take you back to a decade of the Twentieth Century, where you'll relive the years and rekindle the romance of days gone by.

Don't miss a day of the CENTURY OF AMERICAN ROMANCE.

The women...the men...the passions... the memories....

CAR-1

Take 4 bestselling love stories FREE

Plus get a FREE surprise gift!

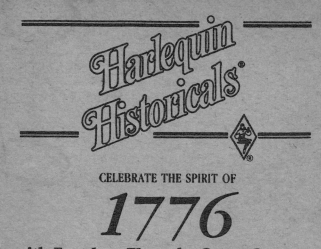

CELEBRATE THE SPIRIT OF

1776

with *Freedom Flame* by Caryn Cameron

Available in July 1990

What better way to celebrate the Fourth of July than with bestselling historical author Karen Harper writing as Caryn Cameron? Freedom Flame is a suspenseful tale of espionage and passion, set during our country's most exciting time—the American Revolution.

Meet George Washington and Benjamin Franklin, Benedict Arnold and John Andre. And, best of all, meet Meredith Morgan and Darcy Montour, who braved the dangers of British-held Philadelphia to spy for the American cause—and found a consuming passion that would bind them together forever.

Every reader will thrill to this sizzling story of the passionate man and woman who helped make our country free.

Only from Harlequin Historicals!

HH48-1

Harlequin Supperromance®

A powerful restaurant conglomerate that draws the best and brightest to its executive ranks. Now almost eighty years old, Vanessa Hamilton, the founder of Hamilton House, must choose a successor.
Who will it be?

Matt Logan: He's always been the company man, the quintessential team player. But tragedy in his daughter's life and a passionate love affair made him make some hard choices....

Paula Steele: Thoroughly accomplished, with a sharp mind, perfect breeding and looks to die for, Paula thrives on challenges and wants to have it all . . . but is this right for her?

Grady O'Connor: Working for Hamilton House was his salvation after Vietnam. The war had messed him up but good and had killed his storybook marriage. He's been given a second chance—only he doesn't know what the hell he's supposed to do with it....

Harlequin Superromance invites you to enjoy Barbara Kaye's dramatic and emotionally resonant miniseries about mature men and women making life-changing decisions. Don't miss:

- CHOICE OF A LIFETIME—a July 1990 release.
- CHALLENGE OF A LIFETIME
  —a December 1990 release.
- CHANCE OF A LIFETIME—an April 1991 release.